CANDLELIGHT

Supreme

"PUT YOUR ARMS AROUND MY NECK AND KISS ME," LOGAN ORDERED.

"I'd rather kiss a pig!" Skylar said to the annoying stranger in the seat next to her.

Logan's eyes became thunderous. "Will you shut up with the claptrap? You'd better cooperate if you don't want us both to get shot."

"What? What are you talking about?"

"That sneaky-looking creature standing over there is after me, and unless we can fool him . . ."

All color drained from Skylar's face as she glanced around the cabin of the airplane. "You mean you aren't just some kind of nut?"

"If you think I'm a nut for wanting to save my neck, then I suppose I am," Logan muttered icily. His arm tightened around her slender frame as he prepared to kiss her. "So unless you want to have my blood on your pretty hands, you'd better do a real convincing job that I'm about the greatest thing to come your way since peanut butter."

CANDLELIGHT SUPREMES

RECKLESS ENCOUNTER

Eleanor Woods

A CANDLELIGHT SUPREME

Published by
Dell Publishing Co., Inc.
1 Dag Hammarskjold Plaza
New York, New York 10017

Dell ® TM 681510, Dell Publishing Co., Inc.

Candlelight Supreme is a trademark
of Dell Publishing Co., Inc.

Candlelight Ecstasy Romance®, 1,203,540, is a registered trademark of Dell Publishing Co., Inc., New York, New York.

ISBN: 0-440-17264-0

Printed in the United States of America

August 1987

10 9 8 7 6 5 4 3 2 1

WFH

To Our Readers:

We are pleased and excited by your overwhelmingly positive response to our Candlelight Supremes. Unlike all the other series, the Supremes are filled with more passion, adventure, and intrigue, and are obviously the stories you like best.

In months to come we will continue to publish books by many of your favorite authors as well as the very finest work from new authors of romantic fiction. As always, we are striving to present unique, absorbing love stories —the very best love has to offer.

Breathtaking and unforgettable, Supremes follow in the great romantic tradition you've come to expect *only* from Candlelight Romances.

Your suggestions and comments are always welcome. Please let us hear from you.

Sincerely,

The Editors
Candlelight Romances
1 Dag Hammarskjold Plaza
New York, New York 10017

RECKLESS
ENCOUNTER

CHAPTER ONE

For one incredible moment Logan Gant stood paralyzed, staring disbelievingly at the crumpled figure on the rough stone floor of the debris-strewn alley. There was little illumination to be found in the bombed-out surroundings, but it didn't take the glare of thousands of lights for him to know the face of his friend.

God!

It simply couldn't be. A mistake, he kept repeating silently—it had to be a mistake. But no matter how hard he tried to convince himself, some gut-wrenching certainty—coupled with the dread that was never far from his thoughts—rocketed into place and assured him that, indeed, it was Achmed: his friend of many years, an accomplice and right-hand man on numerous dangerous assignments, a much valued associate in the game of life and death in which they'd both chosen to participate.

A certain bleakness crept into the rough,

harsh features of Logan's face as he knelt beside the fallen body. He touched his fingertips to the side of Achmed's throat, a burst of hope rushing through him when he felt the faint throbbing of a pulse.

"Achmed!" he exclaimed in hushed tones. "It's me, Logan. Can you hear me?"

It seemed an eternity before there was the briefest flutter of eyelids from the still form. "Logan," he whispered weakly, "I'm so sorry . . . so sorry, my friend."

Logan's hands—which were cradling the increasingly inert body—convulsed with feeling. "You? Sorry? Don't say—"

"Logan," Achmed managed in a surprisingly strong voice. "Please listen. What I have to tell you is of utmost importance. Instead of us leaving Beirut together, using me as a cover—as the plan originally called for us to do—I'm afraid you'll have to get out the best way you can. The mission we were to begin will most likely be put on hold. Something more important is stirring."

"Great!" Logan exploded, casting an uneasy glance over his shoulder. "Nothing about this damned project has made a bit of sense. The communiqué I received told me to meet you here in Beirut at our usual place. That's all. You were suppose to fill me in. Now it's canceled and something else is brewing."

A sudden spasm hit Achmed and contorted his face into a mask of intense pain. A faint trickle of blood found its way from his mouth and began moving down the side of his face.

"Achmed?"

Again there was the tiniest flutter of eyelids. A hand lifted weakly . . . beckoning Logan closer.

He leaned forward, his ear only a whisper away from Achmed's mouth. "Take care, my friend. This—this is a dangerous one. Assassination. Ambassador. Scarab . . . Get to Nicaragua . . . Josh." A fit of coughing turned into a choking gurgle, drawing the last painful breaths from Achmed's body. After one final gasp he slumped, limp . . . lifeless against Logan's large, calloused hands.

The plane was flying quite low over the dense jungle terrain, and in the distance could be seen the approach to the airport. The big man occupying the copilot's seat shifted impatiently. Logan was eager to land. For only then could he see Josh Leighman and find out why someone was tailing him— with his ultimate demise in mind—as well as why Achmed was killed.

An air of steely determination emanated from Logan as he sat next to the pilot in the cockpit of the small plane and tried to decide

13

on a definitive line of action. Achmed's death was weighing heavily on his mind. Twice before he had lost men he'd worked closely with, and twice before he'd sworn he was getting out while he could still walk away. Now . . . . it had happened again, he told himself. Was he next?

Stop it! his inner voice of caution screamed at him. Thinking of your demise is hardly the proper frame of mind to be in when facing the odds you're up against at the moment.

Logan flexed his tense shoulders, straining the faded blue material of the perspiration-stained work-shirt. The khaki pants and dusty three-quarter boots he was wearing were in no better condition than the shirt. In fact, his clothes looked as if he'd slept in them for days —which he had. At least for the last thirty-six hours.

Sleeves rolled back to the elbow revealed hair-roughened forearms, tanned the same dark golden color as his face. A cold, unemotional glint was present in his unyielding gaze —as unnerving to his enemies as it was enigmatic to his friends.

Dark brown hair grew thick against his head and lightly brushed the furrowed skin of his forehead. Heavy brows shadowed sky-blue eyes, which were framed by thick sun-tipped lashes and, at the moment, protected

14

by dark glasses. The tiny lines at the corners of his eyes were the result of the ungodly heat of the Middle East, plus a certain amount of dissipation that had become the norm in Logan's life. His nose was far from a sculptor's idea of perfection, yet it wasn't at all out of place amid the craggy features. Firm lips and an arrogant chin were the final pieces comprising the facial aspect of the man. The composite of several parts, yet revealing nothing of the person behind the far-from-pretty façade.

He was, in his own personal way, mourning the death of his friend. To Logan's way of thinking, that friend hadn't deserved to die in a rubble-strewn alley. At an extreme risk to his own life Logan had managed to get Achmed's body back to relatives.

That had relieved some of the pain. At least till his mind, trained to deal with the most savage acts of man against man, took over by promptly placing the harrowing incidents of the last thirty-six hours into one of the many neat little cubicles of his mind, then pushed another emotional button that told Logan he'd grieved long enough. It was time now to get on with the practices of his trade. Experience and superior training dictated that he do so.

An unexpected lurch of the small plane, as

it began an uncharacteristic swan dive toward mother earth, brought Logan out of his unpleasant reverie. He heard the shrill, whining noise of the single engine and frowned. He wondered what the hell had ever possessed him to board such an aircraft in the first place?—if the pile of junk in which he was a passenger could be dignified by such a name.

He threw a quick, inquisitive glance at the pilot.

A shrugging gesture gave Logan little comfort. "Put your head between your knees and cross your arms over the back of the head for protection," the pilot yelled over the eerie sounds permeating the sweltering interior of the small cabin.

Without bothering to question the wisdom of the advice, Logan found himself trying to do as told. However, his six-foot-four frame was finding it tough going in the close confines. A heavy scowl settled over his rough, angular face, his blue eyes hardening to flinty points as he finally settled for a crouched-over position, his locked fingers clasping the back of his head. He knew better than to brace his body—it was dangerous and stupid. But in that brief millisecond, as the plane approached the treetops and the jungle terrain, Logan did just that. His feet dug in against the metal and his legs became rigid extentions of bone and skin and muscle. His entire body was one continuous line of electrified tension.

The screeching of metal being ripped from its placements filled his ears. That and the peculiar quick snapping sounds. In another brief second of lucidity Logan could only conclude that the belly of the plane was clipping off limbs and treetops like toothpicks as it ploughed an indiscriminate path through the jungle toward some precarious resting place amid the vines and dense growth.

The last thing Logan remembered, just prior to having his body jerked from the plane —through the gaping hole where there was suppose to be metal—and hurled through the air, was the sudden, deafening quiet. But that wasn't possible, he thought rather fancifully the instant before he "embraced" a small sapling. How could silence be such an unpleasant sound?

He failed to find a satisfactory answer, nor could he stave off the wall of darkness descending upon him.

Achmed . . . his untimely death . . . and now, someone tailing him, someone waiting for the right opportunity to kill him . . . the details of this latest mission he was involved in —those thoughts and more ran through Logan's mind.

It was imperative that he remain alert.

However, fatigue and the ungodly beating his body had just withstood won out over sheer determination.

Leaving aside the catnaps on the various aircraft in which he'd been a passenger during the last day and a half, it had been too long since Logan Gant had slept. Too many hours of darting from one spot on the globe to another. Even the prospect of his life being in imminent danger wasn't enough to keep the tall, powerful body erect.

An aura of gentle poise surrounded the petite woman sitting at the head table in the banquet room. Sparkling highlights caught at her short, curly auburn hair. Her green eyes were trained on the speaker in quiet attention, and the understated elegance of the emerald-green suit caressed her soft white skin like the velvet kiss of a lover.

Ankles crossed, hands resting demurely in her lap, Skylar Dennis presented the perfect image of graciousness. Beautiful, grieving . . . but managing to carry on. "Her life torn apart by the injustices that find their way into so many nooks and crannies of society" was how Tim's captain had portrayed her during his address of the convention and while praising Tim, his work . . . and in the end, Skylar.

She looked like a saint.

She felt like the jerk of the year!

The current speaker turned and smiled at Skylar at the conclusion of his talk. She heard the sound of applause, her gaze skimming the sea of people seated at the round tables in the huge room.

For a moment she panicked. Why on earth were all those people staring at her? Could they read her mind? Were they able to discern by simply looking at her that of all the places in the world, this convention of law-enforcement officers was the last place she wanted to be?

True the vocation of enforcing the law was a necessary one, Skylar concluded, extremely necessary. In her position as one-third owner of a restaurant in New Orleans, she appreciated efficient law enforcement. To her way of thinking, however, the people doing the enforcing should agree to remain single. They shouldn't marry and have families. The hazards of the profession created far too much stress and strain on a relationship, thus creating a situation that only served to hurt the two people directly involved.

Unconsciously she fingered the medal before her on the table.

Tim's medal.

She felt like a complete hypocrite. She was *not* the grieving fiancée. In fact, she had been

19

angry as hell at Tim. Angry because he seemed deliberately to choose the most dangerous assignments offered in his department. He had thrived on the undercover operations he participated in, and Skylar had died a thousand deaths each time he began a new case.

When it became obvious that he had no intention of changing, and that her life would become nothing more than continuously teetering on the brink of disaster, Skylar gave Tim back his ring. That it had been the night before he was killed gave her some bad moments—until another officer told her it had been Tim's usual aggressiveness that had gotten him into such a life-or-death situation. He was noted for his impulsiveness. In the end it had cost him his life.

Six months later, when asked by Tim's mother to attend the convention in Dallas where her son was to be honored posthumously, Skylar balked.

"But, Mrs. Dawson, you know Tim and I were no longer engaged."

"Nonsense," the portly woman returned. "I know what my Timmy would have wanted, and that would be for you to go to Dallas and accept this award they want to give in his memory."

"That's an honor reserved for family," Skylar continued to argue. "And while we were all devastated by Tim's death, he and I weren't on the best of terms at the time of his death. In fact, we'd barely been speaking for weeks. I'm not so sure he'd want me accepting his award."

"Well, I'm making the decisions now," Mrs. Dawson reminded her. "You're a good girl, and I say you're the one to go. As a favor to me," she tacked on, knowing to a T how to work the softhearted Skylar.

Sorry, Tim, Skylar offered in silent apology. Whether you like it or not, looks as though I'll be the one doing the honors.

Now she found herself in the unpleasant position of accepting expressions of sympathy from numerous people who thought her to be Tim's bereaved fiancée.

She sighed. As soon as was "respectably" possible, she was going to get the devil out of this gathering, grab the first flight back to New Orleans, place the medal in Mrs. Dawson's plump little hands, then try and forget the entire episode.

Three hours later found Skylar at the airport, just as her flight to New Orleans was announced. She joined the line boarding the plane, carrying her only piece of luggage, a single brown leather bag, on board with her. Hooray for whoever it was that had come up with noncrushable fabrics, she thought idly as she moved down the aisle to her seat.

She opened the overhead compartment and lifted the suitcase over her head just as a huge, bearded, shaggy-haired man with a cane pushed roughly by her, thrust a bag almost identical to hers into the compartment, then promptly dropped into the seat assigned to her.

He was wearing the most outrageous pink-and-green plaid sport jacket, and of all things . . . a black beret. Several gold chains were around his neck and nestled in the dark hair at the V of his rose-colored shirt. Leather pants were snug against long, muscled thighs. Skylar was positive she'd never seen anything uglier or longer than the brown leather sandles that covered his long feet. All in all, she concluded as she completed her frosty perusal of "Mr. Rude," he looked like a clown.

She closed the compartment with a loud bang, then favored the individual with a frosty glare. "Excuse me for being in your way," she said stingingly.

"No problem," the uncouth clod had the nerve to answer in a deep, rough voice that seemed strangely at odds with his bizarre appearance.

Not bad, Logan was thinking as he stared up at the angry blue eyes regarding him as fondly as if a rattlesnake had crawled into her seat, not bad at all. His bold gaze behind the shield of the sunglasses ran appreciatively over the trim, shapely lines of Skylar's body. Good looking . . . good figure. He sure as hell hoped she had a sense of adventure.

"In case you haven't noticed," Skylar said icily, "you're sitting in seat thirteen."

Logan reached into an inside pocket of the atrocious jacket and withdrew the crumpled remains of his ticket. After staring at the bit of information in his hand, he shrugged. "That's right."

"Yes . . . well?" Skylar waited like a small, angry hen whose feathers had been deliberately ruffled. When the great, huge lout showed not the slightest inclination to move, she dropped into the space beside him. Her slender fingers gripped the padded arm separating them, her small bosom heaving with self-righteous indignation. "I demand that you move!" she hissed.

"No."

Green eyes widened in surprise. "What?"

"You heard me. No."

"It's my damned seat, buster." She half turned, catching sight of the flight attendant.

Logan laid a very large hand on her slender arm, his fingers tightening like a vise against the softness of her skin. "I wouldn't do that if I were you."

"Wouldn't do what?"

"Ask for help."

"And why not?"

"Because I'm such a nice person it would be a shame to deprive yourself of my company during the time it takes us to get to New Orleans?" He had the audacity to grin at her.

Skylar took a deep breath, completely out of patience with this absolute idiot beside her. "You are a pain in the behind. Move out of my seat," she said determinedly.

Logan shook his shaggy head. "You are a very stubborn female."

"You don't know the half of it, mister!"

"Why are small women always so belligerent?" he asked pleasantly. "It really isn't fair, you know. Women your size always look so defenseless and all that crap. Yet, when some poor unsuspecting fool—or in this case, a rare gem among men—happens your way, you become hostile. You don't resemble at all the helpless female. More like a tiny whirlwind ready to do me in."

Skylar glowered at him. "That's probably because I don't feel in the least helpless. I also plan on getting the flight attendant and the pilot—if necessary—to help me make you move. Do I make myself clear?"

"There's a man following me, who wants to kill me."

"If there's one thing I can't stand, it's a 'large' man throwing his weight around. As to that wild story, I hope he succeeds within the next few minutes. That way, I can get my seat back without a fuss."

"I lost him in the airport. However, just because I managed to shake him for a few minutes doesn't mean he'll give up. He's mean . . . nasty," he added for good measure, then waited for the outpourings of sympathy.

"So if you aren't out of my seat within ten sec—" Skylar's bottom jaw dropped, her mouth hanging open like a guppy's! Had she heard correctly? Had he said someone was trying to kill him? Certainly not—she all but smiled. Things like that just didn't happen out of the blue. A group of terrorists with bombs . . . that she could believe.

But the longer she stared at the twin orbs of dark glass, the less convinced she became. Before she could stop herself, she reached out and grasped the sunglasses and removed them. She found herself peering into a pair of incredibly beautiful eyes. Dancing blue eyes. How the hell could a person's eyes be dancing when he'd just announced that he was about to be shot?

A con artist could and would say anything, her inner voice of caution reminded her.

"Well, it certainly can't be a jealous husband chasing you, mister," she remarked bluntly, then pushed the glasses back in place. "You have the—er—the plainest face I've ever seen." Even though she was mad as the devil with him, she simply couldn't tell him that he was ugly as sin.

His nose was big, and the beard added nothing to the overall picture. His hair was a nice color, but the ridiculous beret, and the way he wore it scrunched down over his head, hid his hair, and made him look like a mushroom.

As to the business of someone wanting to kill him—well, Skylar mused, some people would go to any lengths to get the window seat. This was one time though . . . She was about to motion to the attendant, when she felt herself being jerked against an iron-hard chest, an arm of steel encircling her upper body.

"Smile and act for all the world as though you find me the most wonderful thing to come into your young life."

Her eyes were wide as saucers, her lips

forming a perfect O as she pressed both hands against the rose-colored shirt in an attempt to free herself. "My God!" she exclaimed. "You do believe in miracles, don't you?"

CHAPTER TWO

"At this particular moment, honey, I'm willing to believe in just about anything," Logan rasped. "Put your arm around my neck and kiss me."

"I'd rather kiss a pig!" Skylar said to the annoying stranger without the slightest hesitation. "I detest beards, not to mention the fact that in this day and age, going around kissing total strangers is an absolute health hazard."

Logan's eyes became thunderous. "Will you shut up with the damned claptrap? You'd better cooperate if you don't want us both to get shot."

"What? What are you talking about?"

"That sneaking-looking creature standing over there is, I think, the one who's after me, and unless we can fool him . . ."

All color drained from Skylar's face. Dear Lord! He really was serious. "You mean you aren't just some kind of neurotic nut trying to get the window seat?" she quavered.

"If you think I'm a nut for wanting to save my neck, then I suppose I am," Logan muttered icily beneath the brilliant smile he was showering upon her. "Smile back at me," he instructed her. "Make it look believable."

Skylar felt the muscles of her cheeks tremble with the effort. "How can it look believable when it isn't?" She inhaled deeply, then just as abruptly let the air out in a hurried swoosh! Her breasts were very intimately pressed against a solid wall of muscle and warm skin, and it was disconcerting as the very devil.

"As attractive as you are, honey, and as nice as your—er—as nice as you . . . feel against me, at the moment I'm more interested in saving my neck than thinking of making love to you," Logan murmured in an irritatingly mocking voice that had Skylar hoping the assassin a successful mission.

"That's about the crudest thing anyone has ever said to me."

"Would you rather I'd jerked away—or murmured a polite 'Excuse me?' "

"It would have been the gentlemanly thing to do."

"There's a time and place for everything, sweetheart," she was told in terse tones. "At the moment, you may think what you damned well please so long as you do as I tell you."

"Isn't that rather nervy of you?" Skylar asked stiffly. Damn his stinking hide, she thought rebelliously, why couldn't he have chosen the tall slinky blonde two rows ahead?

"Do you really think an answer is necessary?" Logan's gaze was steady as he regarded her. Again Skylar was struck by the beauty of his eyes, especially since they were the only redeemable feature in his otherwise ugly face.

"I suppose not." She sighed. "And since I'd do the same for a cat or a dog . . . or even a polecat. Why not an 'ugly-looking,' 'ugly-tempered' beast of a man? At least," she added stonily, "you smell nice and your breath is pleasant."

And he did smell good, she thought crossly, unable to come up with the name of the particular fragrance he was wearing, but liking it nevertheless. It suited him, if anything could suit the man. Airy . . . a bit spicy and clean. It reminded Skylar of wide open spaces. "Are you from the West?"

"Is the exact location of my home a prequesite for you cooperating with me?" Logan all but snarled. He looked around the curling tendrils of auburn hair in which the fingers of one hand were buried, and down the long length of the plane toward the individual who, by then, had moved a few feet down the aisle and was scrutinizing each face. Logan's arm tightened instinctively around Skylar's slender frame as he prepared to kiss her. "Unless you want to have my blood on your pretty hands, you'd better do a real convincing job that I'm about the greatest thing to come your way since peanut butter."

Out of the corner of her eye Skylar followed his gaze. She saw a tall, angular man. His face was expressionless . . . completely, and his head was bald as a billiard ball. She shivered. He fit her idea totally of what an executioner should look like.

After only the slightest hesitation Skylar leaned forward till her mouth was pressing against Logan's. When she would have drawn back, the hand cradling her head exerted pressure and kept her from shifting positions. She felt the tip of his tongue running over the surface of her lips, and became angry.

How dare he take advantage of a situation that was already far and beyond the bounds of reality? "Don't do th—" she tried to murmur, only to have that same marauding tongue plunge inside her mouth. Skylar felt the fine hairs on her nape stand on end as the kiss deepened and became more intimate. Her body took on a tingling sensation that left her deeply puzzled and rather disgusted with herself.

The man holding her in his arms was a total stranger. A stranger in which she'd yet to find even one redeeming quality. Why was his kiss having such a profound effect on her? Why did the captain have to choose that moment to begin taxiing down the runway?

Logan abruptly released Skylar the minute he saw one of the flight attendants speak to the baldheaded man, saw him appear to resist, then watched him angrily drop into a seat in the front of the plane.

A sigh escaped Logan. So his disguise hadn't worked. Or had it? Perhaps with a little extra effort on the part of the woman seated next to him, and a quick exit of the plane upon landing in New Orleans, he just might pull one of the greatest escapes of the century.

His gaze focused far away as he considered the options available to him. He'd been in tight situations during his long years with Orka, but this was one of the most baffling he'd encountered. Always before he'd known or at least had some "idea" who he was fighting. This time, however, he was totally in the dark.

He'd done as Achmed instructed and had flown to Nicaragua for a meeting with Josh

Leighman. Logan rubbed the back of his neck with one hand, his brow furrowing as he remembered the ridiculous plane crash and the absolute comedy of errors that had followed. A crash that had canceled his meeting with Josh and left him still fumbling in the dark. Why were Orka agents the targets of assassins? What had been the meaning of Achmed's garbled dying words?

Now he was stuck on a plane with a man he'd caught several brief glimpses of since his rather hurried departure from Central America, thus giving Logan reason to go with his gut-felt instinct that the man was his enemy. He'd managed to survive in the crazy game of life he played, by learning early on to follow his instincts. He saw no reason to go against that tried and proven adage at this point in his career.

He turned his attention to his newest "partner"—who also just happened to be a very nice armful. Without pausing to consider the gesture, he let his hand, again, touch the auburn softness of her hair. He stared straight into puzzled green eyes and found his conscience pricked by something he saw there.

This is no time for sentimental bullshit, Gant, the cautious, more cynical side of him warned. She was handy, she served your purposes very well, now let it be. When you get

34

to New Orleans, you'll leave her and she'll be none the worse for wear for having helped you.

"You kiss like a twelve-year-old," he said bluntly. Her response had been spontaneous . . . unaffected. It disturbed him.

"If I were as doddering as you are, and if I needed someone as desperately as you *say* you need me," Skylar pointed out in a calm voice, "I seriously doubt I'd be so insulting. And please believe me, you are *definitely* not my type."

"Why did you return my kiss with such . . . ardor?"

"You wanted authenticity, didn't you?"

They stared at each other like two alert, well-armed opponents.

Logan wondered if he had made the remark in a deliberate attempt to hurt her. He rubbed one large hand over his hairy chin. Hell, he wasn't sure why he'd said what he did. Was it because toward the end of the kiss her response had been more than he'd expected? *Was* he trying to hurt her or simply make her aware of how dangerous it was to be so open and honest with her feelings? She was pretty, she looked like a decent person, and he felt about as low as a snake's belly for having used her.

Inwardly Skylar was shocked to the core of

her being. Dear Lord! She'd responded to a perfect stranger in a manner that was—

And a weird stranger at that, her conscience interrupted jeeringly.

Yes . . . well, she tried to reason with the panic rising within her, she was sure the reason she'd "thrown" herself into the role so wholeheartedly was the gravity of the situation.

If you believe that, her conscience continued to harass her, I have some desert property in the Artic I'd like to show you. Ugly as sin or not, there's something about the man that attracts you.

"By the way, my name is Logan Gant."

Skylar gave a start at the low, husky sound of his voice, even though she was still staring at the man. Amazing, she decided, he gives off an entirely different aura than one would normally expect from a man of his type. If he weren't so strange looking, he would be a knockout . . . in a roundabout sort of way.

"Sky . . . Skylar Dennis," she managed on the second try. Damn it all! First he had her kissing him as though he *really* were her lover, and now he had her stammering like she *really* was twelve years old. She wondered what he would come up with for an encore. "Exactly where are you from, Mr. Gant?"

"Here . . . there," he answered. "I travel a lot."

"Oh? Doing what?"

"I'm a spy."

Skylar smiled frostily. "How nice for you. May I sit back in my seat now? This padded armrest has become attached to my ribs."

He'd said he was in danger of being killed, so she'd gone along with his ruse. He appeared to have no home. Now he said he was a spy. And she, Skylar Dennis, was the biggest fool of the year. She'd actually believed him.

"Of course." Logan nodded. "Though I would appreciate it if you wouldn't try moving to another seat."

Something in the way he couched the remark sent a shiver of apprehension over Skylar. "Is that a request or an order?"

He lifted one shoulder indifferently. "An order, though I'd hoped I wouldn't have to say so."

Skylar inhaled deeply, then turned away. The last few minutes had been the most bizarre in her entire life. "Is it necessary for there to be further conversation between us?" She was now positive the man seated beside her was a psycho with some sort of persecution complex. Problem was, how was she to get out of the impossible situation? He could possibly have some sort of weapon on his person.

Even as the thought ran through her mind, Skylar felt her scalp tightening with fear.

"Er . . . care to tell me just who it is you spy for?" She smiled brightly, hoping she looked and sounded convincing.

A mask of bland indifference slipped into place over Logan's features. "I can't reveal the source of my employment. Top secret, you know, and all that stuff."

"Of course." Skylar nodded. Top secret her foot! He was a certifiable nut—not to mention an unpredictable one—and he was all hers from Dallas to New Orleans. That realization left her about as enthusiastic as being hit in the face with a wet rag. During her lifetime she'd found herself in any number of comical and unusual situations. She was impulsive and curious by nature. But this predicament was by far the strangest. What was it Tim always said? "You're the Pied Piper of trouble, Sky, baby. You go together like thunder and lightning . . . you're a walking booby trap."

Well, maybe Tim had been correct in his assessment of her, Skylar conceded, but at this precise moment, whatever he'd thought was of little comfort. She was interested in only one thing, and that was to get the devil away from the hairy idiot, who was now holding on

38

to her hand for dear life. She thought of the baldheaded man she'd seen a few minutes ago. Funny, if he'd really been looking for this Logan Gant character seated beside her, then why hadn't he marched back and forced Gant off the plane? There'd been plenty of time for such a confrontation.

Because your seatmate is dippy as hell, the tiny voice inside her warned. No one is trying to kill him, and the sooner you can let one of the flight attendants know what's happening, the better off you will be.

Unfortunately, as minute by minute into the trip began to pass, Skylar found each move she made effectively blocked by Logan Gant. Every single thing she came up with, he vetoed. It was as if he were reading her mind without the slightest difficulty. She wondered idly if people with an emotional problem were more adept at mental telepathy than others? At any rate, sensible or not, she was surprised to find that she really hated to see the man humiliated.

Well he certainly didn't mind in the least using you, did he? the "voice" asked. And what if he'd singled out some older woman . . . or even a child, for that matter? People like Logan Gant need help. You'd probably be doing him the biggest favor of his life if you'd simply call his bluff, then tell the flight attendants about him so that the authorities could be waiting for him when the plane lands in New Orleans.

Finally deciding that would be the best thing to do with the situation, she looked him steadily in the eye. "Mr. Gant, I honestly think this charade has gone far enough. When I thought you were in danger, I went along with your weird plan. But now that the man you 'imagine' is trying to do you in hasn't even glanced in your direction since he sat down, I'm afraid I find the story more ridiculous by the second. And as to forcing me to remain in this seat till we reach New Orleans" —she lifted one shoulder indifferently—"I know you don't have a weapon on you, so what can you really do? You're having some emotional difficulties right now, but once you get some help, I'm sure you'll be fine."

"There are ways of restraining you, Ms. Dennis, other than shooting or stabbing you."

"Oh, I'm sure there are, Mr. Gant." She smiled coolly at him. "But I don't think you really want to go that far, do you?"

She placed her free hand on the arm of her seat preliminary to rising to her feet, only to have the hand he was holding become imprisoned in a bone-crushing grip.

"Please!" she came close to whimpering as

40

she dropped back in the seat. "You're breaking my hand."

Immediately the pressure was lessened, but he didn't release his hold. "I'm sorry," Logan murmured, then began massaging the skin he'd just treated so roughly. There was an expression of discomfort in the depths of his brilliant blue eyes as he stared into Skylar's frightened brown ones. Dammit, he hadn't meant to hurt her. In fact, the entire scenario made him sick to his stomach. He wasn't a man to hide behind a woman, which was exactly what he was doing at the moment. "I never meant for you to be hurt or involved. I hope you believe me."

"Su-sure." She nodded jerkily. Yet no matter how earnestly he proclaimed his innocence, she was frightened, she was involved, and he had definitely let her know he meant business. Whether or not it was the sensible thing to do, she knew she had no choice but to sit quietly. Perhaps later in the trip something would occur enabling her to escape the watchful eye of her captor. She would stay alert, and when that moment came, she would take advantage of the opportunity.

As they got closer to New Orleans, however, it became patently clear to Skylar that nothing or no one would be able to rescue her from Logan Gant till he was ready to release her. Her hope that one or all of the flight attendants would come to her aid was dismissed when, after the first curious glance in Logan's and her direction, they hid their surprise at the proverbial beauty and the beast, and went about their business.

When they landed in the Crescent City, Skylar looked questioningly at the man beside her. "May I assume my usefulness to you is now over?" She figured it would be far more advantageous humoring his paranoia than pointing out that no one had made the slightest move toward him during the flight.

"Of course." He released her, then flexed his fingers. They felt stiff . . . cramped. "Again I apologize, Skylar Dennis." He smiled as he said her full name, the tiny lines at the corners of his eyes crinkling at the gesture. "You've shown remarkable courage. Most women I know would have been screaming their heads off by now."

"So would I, Mr. Gant, if I hadn't been terrified you would choke me," she returned honestly, a hint of caution still in her voice. "You really should get some help, you know. The next time you do something like this, you may not find as willing a partner."

Logan stood, as well as he could in the tight space. He managed to chuck Skylar under the chin as he squeezed past her drawn-aside knees. "I like your style, honey. Pity we don't have more time to spend together. Maybe some night I'll find myself with nothing better to do. If that happens, then I'll be sure to drop by your place. We can renew old—er—whatever the hell it is that people renew. I do hope you'll forgive me if I insist on leaving first?" God! He shuddered inwardly. He sounded like a first-class ass. However, to his way of thinking, it was by far the most decent thing to do. Skylar Dennis had a kind streak a mile wide. Having her suddenly decide to defend him against some evil force would put her in all kinds of danger.

"Not at all, I—"

Skylar stared disbelievingly at his broad back as he deftly plucked his bag from the overhead compartment, then quickly worked his way through the people and disappeared from sight.

"The nerve of the twerp!"

For a few minutes she simply sat without moving, staring unseeing out the window of the plane toward the busy ground crew bustling about below. The events of the past two days zipped crazily through her mind. She'd actually attended a law enforcement convention, been the recipient of all sorts of sympathetic looks and words, had accepted an award for Tim that should have been received by his mother, and then, on her return to New Orleans, she'd been 'captured' on an airplane—in the presence of nearly one hundred people—and held prisoner during the entire trip.

A drink. She nodded thoughtfully. A . . . damned . . . stiff . . . drink. Yes indeedy, that was definitely what was needed. For only the fuzzy edge brought about by the overindulgence of alcoholic beverage could possibly bring any sort of normalcy—or even a hint of reality—to the recent events in her life.

"Excuse me, miss." The attractive flight attendant smiled down at Skylar. "Is something wrong?"

"What?" Skylar jerked around in surprise; her gaze collided with that of the woman bending toward her, then on to the empty seats lining the cabin. "No . . . no," she shook her head, "there's nothing wrong. Sorry," she murmured embarrassed as she quickly got to her feet, then opened the compartment and took down her piece of luggage.

She looked back at the attendant. "The man"—she moistened her lips—"the man seated next to me. Actually"—she gave a nervous laugh—"he was sitting in the seat assigned to me. He was very obnoxious during the entire flight."

"Really?" The woman smiled. "Funny, we all thought you two were close friends. I mean"—she gestured with her hands, palms up—"you did seem to be enjoying his company. We'd have been happy to assign him another seat if you'd seen fit to complain."

Skylar caught her bottom lip between her teeth, nodding thoughtfully. "Of course," she murmured. "I really should have done that, shouldn't I?" She turned and walked down the aisle, trying to ignore the curious stares of another attendant who had heard the exchange.

CHAPTER THREE

The inability of the driver of the little red car to maneuver smoothly in and out of the murderous rush-hour traffic from the New Orleans airport to an apartment complex in a quiet neighborhood of the city was painfully evident. More than one irate driver's palm became glued to his horn as he prodded the ugly little vehicle on, and Skylar was rattled by unflattering remarks shouted from passing cars. Fits and starts like those of a person with hiccups beset the bedraggled VW on its course. It was old. Its driver's mind was taken over by the imposing face and figure of one Logan Gant.

Logan Gant. Logan Gant.

The name kept reverberating through her mind. She raised her left hand to her temple as if that simple gesture would rid her of the thought of it.

Dammit! Dammit!

The same hand that only seconds ago had

been massaging her temple, banged angrily against the steering wheel. She'd been used. Not just some little old common run of the mill incident. She glared at the traffic before her. No, sirree. She'd been singled out, used, ridiculed, then frivolously dismissed as if the entire incident were of no more importance than a stroll down a quiet neighborhood street. An added insult to injury, she continued to irrationally rationalize, was the lack of conviction she'd found in the flight attendant's eyes while listening to Skylar's story.

Whoa. Stop the jet engines of your unbelievably vivid imagination, the asinine voice reared its obnoxious head. I've yet to see a person switch boats in midstream more than you, regarding this Logan Gant incident. Did you or did you not willingly go along with the man's request to help him further his disguise?

Skylar's small oval chin lifted a fraction of an inch as she grudgingly conceded that she'd done just that. So what? She'd thought he was actually being hounded—possibly threatened —by that awful-looking baldheaded man.

Well, my goodness, Skylar honey, the great wit of her conscience twittered, can the man help it if you, being what you are, swallowed his story like a starving trout gobbling down a gnat? Of course, right after that, you were

48

immediately blessed by a sudden ray of wisdom and decided he was the victim of some sort of mental deficiency. Good for you. *However*, from that moment till now, you've constantly vacillated, with the infamous Mr. Gant going from saint to sinner. Which is it to be, my dear?

"I wish I knew," Skylar quietly murmured. "I wish I knew."

From out of nowhere the tiniest glimmer of a smile began to break through to the full curve of her sensuous lips. An infant dot of brightness became visible in the depths of her dark-brown eyes. These two changes became more and more evident in her features as the ridiculous picture of Logan Gant was revisited in her thoughts.

Suddenly the sound of laughter, warm, low and sparkling, filled the ugly little VW. The driver of the car in the next lane caught a glimpse of her face and smiled to himself. She was pretty—a pleasure to look at. When Skylar glanced his way, she blushed with embarrassment. He lifted a hand in casual greeting, tipped his dark head, then sped away.

She'd been a delightful interlude—bringing a moment of laughter into his world. Now he was gone. Skylar touched the corners of her mouth where the curve of her smile had begun. In and out. That's what Logan Gant had done. He'd entered her life for a brief spell, then vanished. She'd been furious, insulted, and amused by his antics.

And just imagine, Skylar honey, "it" mockingly reminded her, you didn't have to pay a single sou for the entertainment.

And that's that. She nodded pertly. What a story I'll have for Francine.

Approximately an hour later, Skylar sat at the table in the breakfast area of her apartment and watched her closest friend and neighbor, Francine Winter, set two cups of steaming coffee on the table. She'd already called the restaurant and told her partners, Joey and Hubie, that she was back.

"It's the most incredible story I've ever heard," the pretty brunette avowed as she pulled out a chair opposite Skylar and sat down. "Why don't exciting things like that happen to me when I fly?"

"If I ever hear from Logan Gant again," Skylar laughingly assured her, "I'll definitely find out his travel plans and pass them on to you."

After catching up on the past two days' gossip and enjoying another cup of coffee, Francine went back to her apartment and left Skylar to her unpacking.

"A job I detest," Skylar grumbled as she lifted the leather case onto her bed and reached the release to the clasp. She pressed it with her thumb and forefinger. Nothing happened. Again she pressed. Still nothing happened.

"What the devil?" She frowned. After trying a couple more times, she walked over to the antique dresser of cherrywood that had belonged to her grandmother. From the smaller of the two top drawers she removed a ring with several small keys on it. Selecting one, she walked back to the bed, inserted the key into the small hole of the clasp, and turned.

Nothing happened.

Puzzlement was fast turning to annoyance. At that point she began to attack the lock in earnest, and with a number of tools guaranteed to grant her easy access to her clothes and makeup.

In the midst of the battle she was waging against the recalcitrant piece of metal, she noticed that her name and address were missing from the case.

Odd, she mused, fingering the stout leather loop with a plastic-enclosed compartment for name and address of the owner. How on earth could that have happened?

She renewed her efforts to gain admittance to the case. After an especially tough assault with both ice pick and needle-nosed pliers, the lock yielded.

"At last." Skylar exhaled loudly. She'd begun to think she'd have to deliver Tim's medal to Mrs. Dawson, encased in the piece of brown luggage.

The zipper stopped at the end of its metal track. Skylar raised the lid and reached for the silk blouse she knew was on top.

However, instead of finding silk, her fingertips touched rough fabric.

Khaki.

Of all the crazy things to have happened, this was the worst, she thought furiously. Poor Mrs. Dawson. She wouldn't get Tim's medal after all.

Skylar sank to the edge of the bed, an expression of disgust written on her face as she read a laundry label in a shirt. L. Gant. Thanks to Logan Gant she'd endured the embarrassment and total boredom of the convention for naught. She continued sitting on the bed, not even bothering to go through the strange suitcase. That would come later, she decided. At the moment she was too numb.

Numb, yet beginning to see a comical side to the situation. Tim's face floated past the windows of her mind, his expression accusing. "Christ, Sky. My mom sent *you* to accept *my* medal? The poor woman must be totally bonkers." Skylar flopped back on the bed, her laughter filling the apartment.

Time seemed to fly by as Skylar took great delight in going through each and every inch of the detestable Logan's suitcase. Being the neat person she was, she hung the clothes—three shirts, two pairs of pants, and a sport jacket—in her guest-room closet. The underwear, shaving kit, and shoes were left in the case and stored on the shelf of the same closet.

After a lengthy soak in a hot bath Skylar phoned Francine and informed her of the latest development. They laughed, chatted for a moment or two, then hung up. Francine had just gotten in from a date, and Skylar was tired. She made a cup of hot tea and carried it to the bedroom. Once in bed and propped against two fluffy pillows, she turned the lamp on, and slowly sipped the hot drink.

She remembered a story her Aunt Kate used to read to her, about a little girl named Sudy Flower. Sudy Flower was blessed with an imagination of unbelievable proportions. Each day in her idyllic world adventure and daring kept excitement at fever pitch. She slew dragons, sailed ships, defended her castle from the enemy, yet still had time for tea parties with her rag doll, Cassandra, and her dog, Lancelot. At that precise moment Skylar felt remarkably like Sudy Flower.

The last three days of her life had indeed been an adventure. Her eyelids became heavy. She settled the half-finished cup of tea on the bedside table, clicked off the lamp, then slid down in bed, pulling the covers up to her chin. In minutes she was asleep. Asleep and dreaming.

In the dream she was trapped in the land of Feldenflam, between wicked King Gant on one mountain, and rosy-cheeked Queen Sudy Flower on the other mountain. Each day they battled from dusk to dawn, leaving Skylar in the unenviable position of mediator. It seemed to her some member of either of their staffs was constantly knocking upon her door, beseeching her to make peace between the two mountains.

Knocking. Knocking.

She would have to do something about the knocking.

Even in the kingdom of Feldenflam, neither Queen Sudy Flower nor King Gant could still the increasingly annoying hammering.

"Stop it," the sleep-thickened voice muttered.

Knock. Knock.

Skylar's brows stretched upward as far as they could possibly go, her eyes barely slitted as she struggled to catch a glimpse of the lighted dial of the clock beside her bed. One-thirty, she managed to decipher. One-thirty in the morning.

Knock. Knock.

She sat straight up in bed. Aunt Katherine. Something had happened to her Aunt Katherine. "Oh, dear," Skylar began murmuring as she scrambled to her feet, reaching for her robe and pulling it on as she hurried though the apartment to the front door, turning on lights as she hurried along. The "oh, dears" became a rapid litany amid the stern lecture she was heaping upon her head for not having called her aunt the minute she got back. Katherine Damler was Skylar's only family, and they were unusually close. The thought of something being wrong with her aged relative left her trembling with fear.

She reached to unhook the chain, when a shred of common sense prompted her to ask who it was.

The only word she was able to make out was *emergency*. Positive her prior thoughts regarding her aunt were coming true, Skylar flung back the chain and flipped both security locks. "Yes?" she cried out just as she swung open the door. "What's happened to Aunt Katherine?"

"I sincerely hope the dear woman is well and hardy," Logan Gant remarked curtly. One elbow was braced against the doorjamb.

His other hand was tucked inside the horrible pink-and-green plaid jacket.

"You!" exploded from Skylar's lips. Her hands clutched the edge of the door for support. Dear Lord! Had he come back to kill her?

"Nothing so heinous, Ms. Dennis, I assure you," he said cuttingly, then gave a short, humorless laugh when she turned beet-red. She hadn't been aware she'd spoken out loud.

"Wha-what do you want?" she asked tremulously. Her thoughts were in total chaos. Was it possible for her to get to the kitchen, where she could lay hands on a knife?

She looked about sixteen in that thin white robe and matching gown and the tips of her toes peeping out from the bottom. Logan could easily see the two squared necklines, and the pink satin trim that lay protectively against the thrust of her breasts. The sharp outline of the nipples was visible through the soft batiste. The short puffed sleeves lent a certain innocence to the overall effect, yet she looked sexy as hell standing there peeping around the door at him. Her hair was tousled and her cheeks were still warm and rosy from sleep. He remembered how her lips had felt beneath his—remembered her firm breasts pressed against his chest. What it would be like to make love to Skylar Dennis? he asked himself.

"Mr. Gant!"

"Er . . . several things, actually," Logan began, only to be gripped by a sharp pain.

Skylar's eyes widened. His hand inside his jacket seemed to be inside his shirt as well. She wondered why was he holding himself in that odd fashion.

"Oh . . ." She noticed then that there was something even more peculiar about his hair than before. It seemed . . . it seemed . . . No, she assured herself, of course not. However, she tilted her head tentatively to one side and looked hard at the way the beret was slanted across one brow, almost covering one eye. Thing was, she thought with a frown, the hair had followed it. God he was weird! Traveling hair?

"What the hell are you mumbling about now?" Logan snapped. He pushed himself upright, a move that had Skylar edging back sharply, instinctively trying to close the door.

"Oh, no, you don't," he rasped on a painful catch in his voice. He gave one tremendous lunge that brought him and the brown suitcase at his feet into the room, the door slamming behind him. With one hand he fumbled the chain into its groove, then snapped the locks into place. When he turned to Skylar, his expression was grim. "I didn't slip and slide like a damned ferret trying not to be seen getting here, only to have you close the door in my face."

"If you're mad about the luggage," Skylar began, moving backward with all the grace and dignity of a crayfish, "then let me point out that you were the one who left the plane first, Mr. Gant. I refuse to be blamed for the mixup. But I did hang up your pants and your sport jacket. A jacket that I must admit I like much better than the—er—creation you're presently wearing."

"Christ!" Logan exploded. "Don't you ever run down?"

"Not usually," Skylar continued. "And just to set the record straight, sir, I would like to remind you that this is my apartment. You definitely were not invited for a visit. Short or otherwise. I had enough of—"

"Do you have something that will do as a bandage?" he interrupted, without bothering to apologize. At that point he was leaning against the winged side of the Early American sofa. There was a pinched look about his mouth, and his brows were drawn together in a straight, continuous line above the bridge of his large nose.

Skylar paused in her nervous spate to stare crazily at him. The man was insane. Why on earth was he wanting bandages? She lifted one hand disdainfully. "Does this place look like an emergency room?" she asked tartly.

"Unfortunately, no." Logan sighed. He shrugged one arm out of his jacket at that moment, gritting his teeth at the pain even that little amount of movement caused him.

Skylar watched horrified, then became angry. "This is not an airplane, Mr. Logan," she haughtily informed him, forgetting for a moment her fear of the huge man. Frankly, she was tired of him barging into her life. "I can and will call the police if you don't leave this instant!"

"Believe me, Ms. Dennis, nothing would suit me better. I have no wish to involve you in my problems, nor am I finding your company soothing. However"—he inhaled sharply, his face twisted with pain—"at the moment I don't seem to have any other choice available to me. You see, I've been shot."

"Mr. Gant, please," Skylar said impatiently. "First you were being hunted down by an assassin. Next you were—excuse me"—she smiled icily—"*are* a spy. You hold me hostage on the plane. Now you practically break into my home to tell me that you've been shot. Have you ever considered becoming a mystery writer? You certainly have the imagination for it." If she hadn't known him so well, she would have sworn he really was in pain. He had the strangest look on his face. He seemed paler too. Course, she reasoned, in the next few minutes he could also be jumping over small pieces of furniture, trying to convince her he was really a kangaroo disguised as a human being.

Logan, his head bent tiredly, began slowly easing his hand from inside the hideous rose-colored shirt, not knowing if he was reading her correctly or not. He *thought* he could trust her, but circumstances had forced him into such a screwy roll, she might really decide to call the police. He heard her gasp, and quickly looked up at her. She was staring at the handkerchief he had pressed to his side.

"That's blood!"

"Ms. Dennis?" Logan said harshly, ramming the blood-soaked cloth back inside his shirt. She was pale as a ghost, and he had that old gut-feeling she was about to faint. "Skylar? Are you all right?"

As if in slow motion, Skylar raised her head till she was looking straight at Logan. "Of course." She smiled vaguely. "I always faint at the sight of a man bleeding to death in my living room." With those profound words floating past her lips, Logan saw her slight body begin to crumple.

He moved toward her with lightning speed and caught her with his good arm, that last mysterious rush of adrenaline with which all humans seem blessed bursting forth and giving him a spurt of much-needed strength.

After maneuvering her limp body onto the sofa, Logan dropped to the edge and quickly began massaging her arms, shoulders, her face . . . any and all parts of her body his hands encountered. "Damn!" he muttered beneath his breath. "I shudder to think what's waiting for me next."

"Skylar?" He called her name repeatedly, his large hand now clamping her chin and shaking her head. "Skylar? Wake up. Talk to me. You're a fighter, you're not a pantywaist. Argue with me, threaten me." He grabbed her hand, rubbing and patting it, thinking how small and defenseless she really was. He got to his feet and went in search of the bathroom and a cool cloth. All during this brief interruption of his ministrations to Skylar, he kept thinking: small and defenseless.

And you've involved her in a situation that could very well cause her physical harm . . . possibly even . . .

No! Logan turned pale beneath the deep tan. No. Nothing must happen to her . . . nothing would happen to her. He'd see to that. He patted her face with the wet cloth,

61

then rubbed it against her cheeks till they were apple-red.

Christ! Wasn't she ever going to wake up? Maybe he should call someone.

"Will you please stop scrubbing my face?"

A crooked grin hovered over Logan's stern mouth, giving him a faintly rakish look. "Coming around, Ms. Dennis?" He was holding her hand, and he didn't seem in the least hurry to let go of it. A huge breath of relief fluttered noisily past his lips. "You had me worried for a few minutes, kiddo."

"Good! You scared me out of ten years' growth, mister." She stared at him for several tingling seconds. "Two questions, Mr. Gant."

"Shoot," he agreed, finding himself enormously pleased that she was herself again and all starch and vinegar with him.

"How on earth is it possible for your hair to move around on your head, and how did you get shot?"

CHAPTER FOUR

Logan reached up and grasped the beret.

An astonished "I don't believe it" burst from Skylar's lips as she observed the beret, and the wide fringe of dark hair sewn to the edge, dangling from his fingers. "Where on earth did you get such a thing?"

"From an aspiring thespian." He further amazed her by removing the full beard that covered the bottom half of his face. Afterward he ran long fingers through his own dark brown hair that had been pressed thick and flat against his head.

The transformation was amazing. "I can't believe the difference," Skylar murmured in an awed voice. He could never be called handsome, but the strength and authority she saw stamped in his features was magnificent. Only one flaw remained. "I take it the nose isn't a prop?"

Logan stared haughtily at her down his very prominent appendage. "I'll have you know this nose is the Gant heritage, Ms. Dennis," he said, the twinkle in his eyes belying the chilly tone of his voice.

"My only comment to that is, God bless you, Mr. Gant. You indeed have a heavy cross to bear." She asked, on a more serious note, "What about your wound?"

"I assure you it's still very much in evidence, Ms. Dennis."

"Are you running from the law?"

He tipped his head to one side and regarded her with open speculation. "Would it matter to you if I were?"

"It would matter . . . yes. I would hate for that to be the case. And, being the sort of person I am, I suppose I would call the authorities . . . once you're on your way, of course. In the meantime, however, it wouldn't stop me from offering you the use of my bandages and some of my antiseptic. So, are you running from the law?" she asked again.

"I'm not running from the law. In fact, you *could* stretch your imagination and say I'm part of the law myself." He chewed thoughtfully at his bottom lip for a moment. "At this particular time, however, it's not prudent for me to go to the police. My particular—er—'group' and the police usually don't work together."

"Spy," Skylar whispered, the hair on her

arms rising. An eerie quietness settled in the confines of the room. This was very unnerving. Her eyes narrowed as she stared at him. "You weren't kidding when you told me you were a spy, were you?" Dear Lord! How could this be happening to her?

"I'll admit that at the time, I threw it into the conversation just to throw you off stride. But yes, I suppose you could call me a spy."

For several electrified moments there was total silence as their gazes merged and their thoughts had a field day of activity. Each seemed to be searching out the physical and mental endurance of the other, measuring, wanting to trust, yet afraid of disappointment.

"If you'll let me get up, Mr. Gant," Skylar suggested, breaking the awkward silence, "I'll see what I can unearth in the way of bandages. Better still, shouldn't we get you to a doctor?"

"A doctor would entail an explanation— and complications, Ms. Dennis. I'd prefer to wait till I've made a phone call."

"There's a phone in the kitchen and one in my bedroom. Why don't you use the one in the kitchen, while I see about bandages and antiseptic," Skylar said matter-of-factly.

It was a dream, she kept repeating to herself. Like Sudy Flower, dreams and fantasy were for everyone . . . just for the asking. She kept pushing to the back of her mind the unsettling conclusion that her life had taken an important turn without her ever having been aware of its having moved. Frankly, she was terrified of dreams and fantasy.

Logan walked a little unsteadily to the kitchen, found the phone, and punched in the numbers that would give him Allen Deen, Orka's chief, then waited for the electronic voice scrambler to kick in.

"Hawk here," he said quickly the minute the programed click sounded. Code names were always used during any type of telecommunications, and the habit came as easily to Logan as breathing. He was an excellent agent—through and through. It was his life.

"Thank God!" Allen Deen exclaimed the moment he heard the deep, rugged voice. "These past forty-eight hours have been pure hell." He dropped back in his chair, literally quivering with relief, his fingers edging inside his collar in nervous reaction. Logan Gant was more than just an agent with Orka. He and Allen were friends. Due to Achmed's death Allen already had closed one corridor within the last two days. He'd been sweating the hours, hoping against hope that he wouldn't have to close the second one, especially that one belonging to the Hawk.

66

"Hasn't been exactly a picnic from my end, Rainbow. Fill me in on what the hell's going on. Nothing's gone right from the minute I found Achmed in that damned alley. Where the hell is Raven?"

"Of course you know about Phoenix. Raven was wounded rather seriously, so that added to the confusion—the two of you being unable to make connections in Nicaragua. Rumors are flying like crazy, Hawk. The long and short of it is, it looks as though somebody is putting a lot of pressure on our agency. The person applying that pressure appears to be an expert in the field of eliminating people and terrorizing in general. It would seem we're not at all well liked. Doesn't that just tear you up?" he asked mockingly. "There are two or three trains of thought as to why we're suddenly so popular, but at the moment nothing concrete. What's your location and outlook?"

"Sector eleven. Confusion. Probable wounding of one hostile agent, whereabouts of his partner unavailable. Both parties unknowns. That fits with Orka's momentary inability to identify said parties. Particulars to follow via usual course," Logan told him, then gave Skylar's phone number in a peculiar gibberish code that had, so far, proved unbreakable.

67

"Personal update?"

"Flesh wound above the waist on right side."

"Are you sure it's just a flesh wound, Hawk?" There was concern in Allen's voice. If the Hawk had been wounded, then things were really bad. He was Orka's best agent. Anyone able to get to him had to have been extremely clever.

"Positive. Don't worry. I'm not anxious to leave this world yet."

"Take some time off and let that wound heal. God knows you've accumulated enough. Once you're fit, it would be a good idea to try and find out more about your assailant. Offhand, I'd say your best bet is to stay right where you are."

"That may present a small problem."

"Oh?"

"The person helping me has been unwittingly included in this mix-up. I'm not sure they'll want to continue."

"Male or female?"

"The latter."

"And you're telling me you've lost your powers of persuasion?" Rainbow teased. "You, who've always had members of the opposite sex pampering you like a baby, ready to do your slightest bidding?"

"Mmmm, yes, well," Logan hedged, "I'm

68

afraid this . . . person isn't quite as malleable as others of my acquaintance have been."

"Good for her." Allen laughed. "If the situation weren't so critical for you, I'd wish the lady luck. By the way, as soon as I get additional information from you, I'll be sending Cochise to help you."

"Thanks, he's a good man," Logan remarked dryly. "Now, what about the 'project' I was to start on?"

"It's been canceled, so until we get a better handle on things from this end, do yourself a favor and get some rest. You sure as hell deserve it."

"I'll remind you of that remark when you call me in the middle of the night and tell me I'm needed in Pakistan. See ya, Rainbow." Logan cradled the receiver, then slowly turned and stared straight at Skylar, who was standing still as a statue just inside the doorway. There was very little color in her cheeks, which emphasized the emerald-green of her large, frightened eyes. The softly veiled panic reflected in her gaze reminded Logan of a cornered doe.

Earlier, when the two of them had been sitting on her sofa and he'd reluctantly confirmed he was a spy, the confession hadn't really hit Skylar. She was still punchy from his screwy behavior during the Dallas-to-New

Orleans trip. Add her shock at seeing him again so soon, not to mention the wild and crazy dream from which she'd been awakened by his heavy pounding on her front door, and she was dang nigh a candidate for the funny farm. But when she'd walked into the kitchen and heard him talking, the dreadful implications of his profession and the price it required of a person brought all her conflict with Tim rushing to the fore.

She really didn't want to appear callous, she lectured herself, but as soon as the man was taken care of and on his way, the happier she would be. She shivered. For some unknown reason Logan Gant's very presence brought with it the threat of disaster.

"Who is Rainbow?" Her voice sounded strange even to her own ears, high-pitched and scratchy.

Logan leaned against the edge of the counter. He was weary and exhausted, and the wound in his side was beginning to hurt like hell. Yet, in spite of the rush of impatience at her question, he found himself feeling a strange obligation to set this woman's mind at ease.

His motivation, however, wasn't completely unselfish. Her cooperation was something he desperately needed at the moment —and in the days to come. There'd been times in the past when he'd been forced to place his life in the hands of total strangers. In that sense, this instance was no different from all the others. Though it was nice, he reflected ruefully, that his rescuer at the moment was a beautiful woman. On the other hand, beautiful or not, he knew he had no other choice than to trust her. "Rainbow is the code name for the head of the agency with which I'm associated. It had been nearly three days since I'd checked in, and I knew the staff would be concerned."

"What would have happened if they hadn't heard from you by tomorrow?"

"It would have been assumed I was dead. My official corridor would have been closed, my code name destroyed. In short, the Hawk would have ceased to exist, Ms. Dennis."

Hawk. How appropriate, Skylar thought. It suited him to a T. Lean and tough and predatory, and with a certain arrogance. The image the name conjured up was perfect. "Is that the usual procedure?" she asked in a barely audible voice, her fingers unconsciously stroking the raveled edges of the white cotton material she was holding. Why on earth was she asking so many questions? she wondered.

He shook his head, an impenetrable mask slipping into place over his face. "One of our agents in Beirut, a good friend of mine, was

71

killed two days ago. I just learned that another one in Central America has been wounded."

"And you've been wounded."

Logan shook his head. "So I have."

"It could have been you in Beirut, couldn't it?"

Why the hell was she being so curious? He was in pain. At the moment all he wanted was the chance to drop someplace and sleep. Logan's eyes narrowed speculatively. He was accustomed to reading people, and Skylar Dennis was no exception. He began to discern more than the usual curiosity in that lovely face, in her voice, and in the rigid stance of her body. She was a woman in pain, he decided shrewdly, emotional pain. "It could have, but it wasn't."

"Do you ever think about dying?" Skylar asked on a sudden rush of exhaled air, then wished she could take back the words. What on earth had possessed her to ask such a thing?

"If you don't mind," Logan suggested, eying the articles in her hands, "I'd like to see to my wound. Afterward, I'll be happy to discuss with you some of the hazards of my profession."

Skylar felt the embarrassed warmth of a flush steal over her cheeks. Dear Lord, how could she have been so thoughtless? From the look of the man's face he appeared to be in intense pain.

"Forgive me, Mr. Gant. Please," she hurried over to the small table for two in the kitchen and pulled out a chair. "Sit down." She deposited the antiseptic bandage material on the table, then found a small plastic pan beneath the sink and filled it with warm water.

As he sat down, and with only a minimum of difficulty, Logan unbuttoned his shirt and eased it off his shoulders. He looked up at the hovering, white-faced Skylar, one large hand holding the shirt over the jagged tear in his skin. "This isn't necessary, you know," he said softly.

There was no ridicule in his deep voice, and for that she was thankful. "Please," she said so quietly, he could barely make out the word. "I need to do this. You aren't the only one with your ghosts and secrets, Mr. Gant."

Logan inhaled deeply, then released the shirt, his blue eyes alert for the slightest sign that she was going to be sick or faint. Instead, he watched her take a deep breath, saw her small hands clench into tight fists, then watched her take the final step to his side.

But as she worked at cleansing the wound, then applying the medication and later a bandage, Skylar wondered if she wouldn't have

73

been wiser to have let him take care of himself. She'd never seen a chest so thick or so tanned or so . . . She envisioned her face nestled against the hair-roughened wall, her fingers idly trailing through the luxurious dark growth. Quick, inquisitive glances were directed toward gorgeously wide shoulders and forearms that left little doubt of his physical prowess. His body—what she could see of it—was the epitome of strength, yet wasn't overly big. Perfectly formed bone structure . . . muscle flowing into muscle . . . creating a tone of balance that struck Skylar as unique and beautiful.

Ten minutes later she glanced briefly at her patient's face. Seated, his head was just a little bit lower than hers. For the first time she noticed the heavy film of perspiration on his forehead. Without thinking she blotted the moisture from his skin, then stepped back. "You can breathe now, Mr. Gant. I've managed to get through it without falling all over you in a dead faint."

Logan glanced down at his side and saw that the area was now neatly bandaged. He looked up at Skylar, observing that her color still wasn't what it should have been. "And very nicely, I might add. Thank you, Ms. Dennis. Now I have another favor to ask of you."

"Oh?" Skylar asked while she tidied up the mess she'd made.

"Due to certain circumstances totally beyond my control," he began to explain, "I find it—er—shall we say, extremely prudent to remain out of sight for several days. I managed to shake my friend from the plane, and his friend, who apparently was waiting for him here in New Orleans."

"So?" She eyed him critically. Surely he wouldn't, she thought.

"I need a place to stay for a few days. And unless there's someone in your life who would object, I'd like to stay here."

Skylar was convinced her hearing had gone haywire. She looked sharply at him for a moment, then finished her cleaning up, positive that absolute clarity of thought and sound would shine upon them, and she could forget what she thought she'd just heard. "I've never considered myself as needing a hearing aid, but I suppose anything is possible," she even went so far as to mutter to herself.

"There's nothing wrong with your hearing, Ms. Dennis," Logan exhaled on a long, tired breath. He regarded her with eyes as hard as steel points. "I apologize for having involved you in the first place, but I did, and nothing on earth can change that. I hate to be melodramatic, but my life is at stake, and quite frankly, I don't exactly care to give that bald-headed bastard and his associates the pleasure of executing me."

"Oh, God!" Skylar shuddered. She crossed her arms at her waist, her palms cupping her elbows. "You're really serious, aren't you?" she whispered.

"Dead serious," Logan answered roughly.

"And if I refuse to let you stay? What then?"

Logan shrugged one shoulder, then immediately winced from the pain even that slight movement had caused him. He silently cursed the woman standing before him and the situation that had placed him in such a precarious position. He resented like hell being at another person's mercy. It went against his makeup. "I'm not omnipotent, Ms. Dennis," he remarked dryly. "However, we both know I didn't shoot myself, I didn't imagine the man on the plane or the telephone conversation you heard a few minutes ago. In light of such evidence, I'd venture to say someone out there seems to be in a damned sweat to relieve this earth of my presence."

"I'm not some child, or so stupid, Mr. Gant, that you have to enumerate each and every misadventure you've endured since we met. But since you did feel the need to be so insulting with your explanation, I'll try to return the favor. As you've probably guessed by now,

I do live alone—by choice, I might add. But before you get any ideas that that automatically solves the question of your residence for the coming days, I'd like to point out that I don't like spies."

Added to the fear and astonishment seeping over her entire being was now a healthy dose of anger. How dare he implicate her— even remotely—in the covert activities that governed his life. How on earth was it possible, she asked herself for the umpteenth time, for her to have been engaged to a man involved in a career she detested, and now to find herself literally saddled with a wounded spy?

"Just why do you dislike spies so badly, Ms. Dennis?" Logan asked curiously.

"Oh"—Skylar gestured frustratedly with her hands, her voice agitated—"I don't dislike 'spies' in general, Mr. Gant. It's the conditions of your profession that I detest. . . . That, and other aspects of the tradition that causes a man to always consider the almighty job first —a very dangerous job, I might add—then allows him to 'justify' putting his family and . . . anyone else of importance in his life, second." She glared at Logan. "Have you ever been in the position of knowing that the person you love would rather be dressed in some sleezeball garb, living 'undercover' with gutter lowlife, than having dinner with you in some nice restaurant or even making love with you?"

"No," Logan replied in a calm voice, "I can't honestly say I have. Has that happened to you, Ms. Dennis?"

"Yes it's happened to me, Mr. Gant," Skylar snapped. "It happened to me with my fiancé, who was an undercover detective. It destroyed our relationship."

There was the barest nod to Logan's dark head as he digested this information. So . . . he silently mused, now he knew the reason for that expression he'd seen earlier. A weird sense of helplessness swept over him as he considered Skylar's explanation and the bitterness in her voice. There'd been pain, resentment, present. It was as if he felt her pain, and that puzzled him. He wondered about the absent fiancé. How could a man in his right mind walk away from any sort of relationship with a woman like Skylar Dennis?

"Perhaps the two of you weren't suited for each other, and your fiancé's career merely became the whipping boy for incompatibility," he offered.

"Horse muffins!"

Logan's eyes rounded with amusement and his lips quirked with suppressed laughter. "I beg your pardon?"

78

"You know exactly what I mean, Mr. Gant." Skylar pinned him with a "meaningful glower." "My fiancé chose to dedicate himself to his lousy job with a singlemindedness that bordered on insanity."

"Come, now, Ms. Dennis." He smiled condescendingly . . . or so it appeared to Skylar. "Are you such a prima donna that you would expect the man in your life to be at your beck and call twenty-four hours a day?"

"Don't be an ass, Mr. Gant," he was told unceremoniously. "Tim wasn't the sort to be henpecked, nor am I so immature as to want that kind of power over any man. However, I didn't think it unreasonable to want to spend at least one evening a week with my fiancé. Nor did I think of myself as being a prima donna to want to have dinner once in a while or even go dancing occasionally."

"Perhaps—er—Tim is a trifle gung-ho when it comes to his work," Logan suggested, trying to temper the hostility he saw in Skylar's green eyes. Personally, he considered this fellow Tim to be dumb as hell.

"Was, Mr. Gant, was."

"I beg your pardon?"

"Tim 'was' gung-ho. So much so, he went rushing off one evening and got himself killed. Needless to say, I'm not very sympathetic to a profession—regardless how law abiding—that's caused me so much pain. In my opinion the whole schmear stinks.

CHAPTER FIVE

Nothing in Logan Gant's rather turbulent thirty-nine years had quite prepared him for the fiery-eyed, auburn-haired beauty standing glaring at him, her fists jammed against her hips. In spite of the anger stiffening her small, slender body, he discerned a pathetic vulnerability emanating from Skylar. Pathetic in the sense that she'd been deeply hurt, but still seemed puzzled as to why.

"I'm sorry," he said after an awkward silence. He watched her quickly turn and begin wiping—again—an already clean counter top, while trying to cope with the embarrassment brought about by her outburst.

"No," she finally managed. "I'm the one who should be apologizing."

She turned and faced him. Dear Lord! Why in heaven's name had she suddenly become so hostile? Why did it matter to her what the crazy man did for a living? And why was she finding it so incredibly easy to stare at his bare chest, when she should have been looking him in the face? "I shouldn't allow past mistakes to dominate my thinking. Though to be perfectly honest, I find your profession to be . . . shall we say, a necessary evil, but still an immensely uncomfortable one?"

"I appreciate your candor."

"How long do you think you need to stay out of sight, Mr. Gant?" Skylar asked abruptly, dragging her eyes upward to meet his unreadable blue ones. It wasn't a situation she was eager to become a part of. On the other hand, considering his physical condition, she could hardly push the man out the door.

You sap! What if he's not a spy, but some kind of homicidal maniac? . . . even a deranged sex offender? her fertile imagination quickly pointed out.

Skylar all but laughed out loud as the ridiculous thought raced through her mind. The man was positively nodding in his chair from exhaustion, not to mention the evil-looking wound in his side. She seriously doubted Logan Gant had been so taken with her during the flight from Houston that he was simply waiting around for an opportunity to jump her frightened bones.

"How long, Mr. Gant?" she repeated, then did a double take when she discovered his eyes closed and his head leaning against the top rung of the ladder-back chair. He was sound asleep!

Without hesitating Skylar hurried from the kitchen, down the hall, and into the guest room. She stood at the foot of the single bed, chewing pensively at her bottom lip. Her guest was a big man. Her bed was made for a person built on far less generous lines than Mr. Gant. Beggars can't be choosers, she pacified herself, then darted out into the hall to the linen closet for clean sheets.

No sirree, she continued the silent litany as she made up the bed. When one invited himself to another's home, then it stood to reason one should expect to compromise a certain amount of his comfort.

Well, her conscience sounded off, judging from the size of this bed, compared to the size of the 'one' who will be sleeping in it, one should expect to be as uncomfortable as holy hell!

Without giving herself time to speculate further on the infamous Mr. Gant's comfort, Skylar rushed back to the kitchen. After seeing that he was still asleep and beginning to snore like a steam locomotive, she stood uncertainly in the middle of the room. Was he one of those people who came up swinging when awakened abruptly?

She took a tentative step closer. "Mr. Gant?" She cleared her throat, took a deep breath, and walked right up to him. "Wake up, Mr. Gant. You're much too large for me to carry to bed, you know." One slim hand went out and touched his shoulder.

Before Skylar could blink an eye, she found her wrist manacled in a grip of iron and twisted in such a manner as to force her across the lap of Logan Gant. His other hand was at her throat, his fingers spread like deadly talons, waiting to squeeze the life from her body.

Dear sweet heaven!

Skylar stared incredulously into the rigid mask of humanity hovering over her. She saw such a cold, dedicated force struggling for survival, it alone made her shiver. The hand at her throat—and the strength in it—telegraphed that same message to her brain about the same time that she managed to whisper Logan's name in a barely audible voice.

"Please. You're hurting me."

Immediately the hand left her throat, and the grip on her wrist was loosened. But instead of letting her get up, Logan dropped an arm across her thighs, pinning her to him. His gaze was enigmatic as he held her against the uninjured side of his chest. "I'm sorry, Skylar Dennis," he rasped huskily.

A finger gently touched the red spots that already were marking her throat. "In my particular line of work, being abruptly awakened can cause problems."

"Y-you can say that again," a shaken Skylar croaked, trying to swallow the huge lump of fear lodged in her throat. Jesus! With only a teensy-weensy bit more pressure on her throat, she'd have been dead as a doornail by now.

A ghost of a smile slitted across Logan's craggy face. "Next time, throw water on me. Okay?" Skylar nodded, still shaken, then watched with eyes as round as saucers while his mouth came closer and closer to hers.

Merciful heavens! He was going to kiss her.

She lay as passive as a rock. Not a muscle moved while sensuous lips touched and nibbled at hers, while the hot tip of a tongue traced and teased with all the freedom of a lover. After what seemed like an incredibly short but explosive time, Logan raised his head, his gaze curious.

"You responded better the first time I kissed you, Ms. Dennis."

"That was before you tried to throttle me, Mr. Gant." She smiled frostily. "Somehow having a man choke me one minute, then kiss

85

me the next, leaves me rather unmoved . . . if you get my drift."

"Point taken. I'll remember that in the future."

"Don't bother, Mr. Gant. I can assure you our futures won't have the slightest effect on each other."

Logan continued to study her, still puzzled by the feelings this woman stirred in him. Ever since he'd met her on the plane, there'd been moments when she reminded him of . . . It was the silliest damned thing in the world, he harshly concluded before memories could inflict further pain. He released her and joined her as she pushed herself to her feet. "Stranger things have happened, Ms. Dennis, stranger things have happened."

Skylar didn't answer as she gained her footing and sought to retain some small part of her dignity. There was no point trying to trade off insults, she told herself. Besides, his last remark was ambiguous to say the least. She was fairly certain he wasn't speaking entirely of his conduct.

"If you'll follow me, Mr. Gant, I'll show you where you'll be sleeping."

Logan watched the gentle sway of her slim hips beneath the thin material of the robe as they walked from the kitchen to the guest bedroom. Careful, Gant, his voice of caution mocked him. This one is tricky. She's leery of men in your particular line of work, she's sharp tongued as hell, yet she's as warm and delightful an armful as you've ever held. Any more tricks like the one you pulled back there in the kitchen, and she could quite easily become another of the numerous problems dotting your life.

The minute Logan clapped eyes on the single bed, he all but groaned out loud. Men of his size had long since outgrown a bed constructed for midgets. "Er . . . nice." He smiled weakly at a hovering Skylar. "Where is the bath?" Half dead, both legs broken, or merely tired, he never went to bed without a shower. That is, he quickly amended, unless he was being chased by some gun-happy ass ready to shoot him.

"Through there." Skylar nodded toward a door. "I'm afraid we'll be sharing."

"Don't worry." He grinned. "I'm disease free, and I promise to clean up after myself."

"Good. I detest housework."

"Do you cook?"

Skylar sighed. "I do, but in my line of work, cooking for pleasure doesn't happen too often." It was the silliest conversation she'd ever had. She was relating personal preferences as if he were a good friend.

"Exactly what is your particular line of

work, Ms. Dennis? By the way," Logan continued on before she could answer. "Considering the uniqueness of our situation, don't you think it would be better if we dispensed with Ms. Dennis and Mr. Gant?"

"I suppose it would make more sense," Skylar admitted. "And to answer your question, I'm one-third owner in a restaurant."

"Ahh." Logan nodded. "So that accounts for your not wanting to cook when you get home."

"Perhaps, Mr. G—er . . . Logan. Perhaps I've missed something. Exactly how long do you think it will be necessary for you to hide out here?"

"Already eager to get rid of me, Skylar?" He dropped on a chair the shirt he'd been holding, then flexed the muscles of his uninjured shoulder. "May I get that shower now?"

"Certainly." Skylar turned and walked to the door, feeling much the same as a child who has been dismissed. "You'll find your clothes hanging in that closet." She motioned toward the louvered doors to the right of the bed. "I left the shoes, shaving kit, and underwear in the case. It's also in the closet—on the shelf."

Later, after Skylar had returned to bed, she found sleep to be as elusive as a butterfly. Lord! Of all the scrapes she'd gotten into during her lifetime, and there had been plenty, this had to be the wildest of them all. What on earth was she going to tell Francine?

For that matter, what are you going to tell your Great-Aunt Katherine? her conscience probed.

Skylar buried her face in her pillow and groaned. Her aunt was difficult to handle when things were going smoothly. It would be pure hell over the next few days if Katherine Damler got wind of a strange man living in her niece's apartment.

Eventually Skylar went to sleep with a tiny grin on her lips, as visions clipped through her mind of her tiny, white-haired aunt wielding a huge club in hot pursuit of a fleeing Logan Gant.

The next morning Skylar was awakened to the smell of coffee and frying bacon. She rolled over onto her stomach, her eyes still closed, and her nose twitching.

Bacon? Coffee?

Was she losing her mind? Could she have possibly walked in her sleep, cooked an entire breakfast, then gone back to bed?

At that moment there was the distinct sound of a dish breaking, followed by a smothered "Damn!"

Ahh. Skylar sighed, her breath hot against her arm as memories of what transpired the night before ran through her mind. She wasn't sure whether she should be thankful she hadn't taken to nocturnal wanderings or that the aroma and sounds were caused by the totally male person making himself very much at home in her kitchen. Either choice was far from a pleasant one.

Ten minutes later, clad in a pink robe, Skylar entered the kitchen, her stomach rumbling with hunger.

"Good morning," she brightly announced to the bare back of her guest, who was clad only in dark pants. When she realized that he held the dustpan in one hand and the broom in the other, and was attempting to clean up a broken plate at his feet, she hurried forward. "For goodness sake, let me have that broom before you cut your feet to ribbons or cause your wound to start bleeding."

"No, thank you," she was curtly told. "I'm not an invalid, Skylar, I can manage."

"Well, excuse me," she threw right back, promptly sticking out her tongue toward his broad back at the exact same instant he turned and looked at her. She'd hoped a few hours sleep would help rid her mind of the perfectly foolish notion that he was—without a doubt—the sexiest man she'd ever met. Unfortunately, a full frontal view of chest and shoulders, even with a huge bandage on one

90

side, was devastating. Why couldn't he have been wrinkled as a prune and ninety years old?

"Oh, dear." He grinned evilly. "Did I hurt your feelings?"

With an embarrassed toss of her auburn head Skylar walked over to where the coffee was waiting and poured herself a cup. "Certainly not. Why should I care if you abuse your body and have to camp out here days longer? I just *adore* having a total stranger bumbling around in my apartment." She smiled sweetly at him, but her eyes were far from warm. "When I think of the other prospects your presence brings, I can barely contain myself. Why—there's something positively rejuvenating about taking a guest for a stroll along the street and having someone shoot at him."

"Someone shot at one of your guests?" Logan asked alertly, remembering Allen saying something about her being involved in different sorts of protesting.

"No," Skylar snapped, thinking him dense as a post. "But from what you've told me, they sure as hell will take a shot at you if you dare show your ugly face."

"Other than you and my agency head, no one knows I'm here, Skylar. There are ways of losing a tail," he explained patiently. The remains of the plate were dropped into the garbage. He put the broom and dustpan back in the utility closet, then turned to her again.

Skylar dropped into a chair at the table and stared moodily at him. "Which I'm sure you know all about, don't you?"

"Well, of course I do, honey," he remarked facetiously. "Otherwise I wouldn't be standing here in your kitchen, gazing into your lovely, smiling face."

"May I point out that you started this little battle by being so nasty when I offered to help you?" she pointed out to him.

"Then the next time I break a dish, I'll be sure to accept your help. Will that make you happy and give you peace of mind?"

Skylar refrained from answering, simply because there was no point in repeating herself. Peace of mind, as long as Logan Gant was around, was out of the question.

Conversation after their rather cryptic exchange was brief. While she ate breakfast, Skylar answered several questions, then gave Logan her telephone number at the restaurant. Later, as she was leaving the apartment, she also had him jot down Francine's number.

"Just in case something happens and you need someone in a hurry."

"Perhaps something *will* happen while you're gone, Skylar. That way, you'll be rid of my distasteful presence and get your place all to yourself in one fell swoop," Logan remarked mockingly.

Skylar opened her mouth to protest such a suggestion, but thought better of it. "Well, if you see that you're about to be shot or stabbed or whatever, please see if you can get them to 'do you in' in the corridor and not in my living room. It might leave a stain on my carpet. Bye now."

"You've got to be kidding." Francine shook her head disbelieving. "You honestly expect me to believe you have a real, honest-to-God spy stashed away in your apartment?" They were having lunch at a secluded corner of Hubie's, so named for one of the three owners.

"Logan Gant, in the flesh. I can't wait for you to meet him, Francine. He's different from any other man I've ever known."

"How different?"

Skylar gazed past her friend toward the profusion of greenery in hanging baskets on the patio, visible through the multipaned window by their table. "I get the distinct impression that he's playing with me. Kind of like a huge cat, watching and switching his tail back and forth right before he pounces and enjoys a fat juicy bird for dinner."

Francine laughed. "You're nuts. Seriously,

93

though, are you saying that you don't think the situation is as serious as he's told you?"

"Oh, no." Skylar quickly shook her head. "I believe him on that score. It might not have been the nice thing to do, but I eavesdropped on his conversation last night, when he called his agency." She shrugged one slim shoulder. "From what I could hear him saying and from his responses to his boss, it seems something very frightening is going on within the agency."

Francine leaned forward. "Does he know you heard his conversation?" she asked in a conspiratorial whisper.

"Partly. I walked on into the room just as they were finishing. I don't mind telling you, I'm having mixed emotions about having him in the apartment."

"That's understandable. Yet, only minutes ago you were telling me how different, how appealing, he is," the brunette pointed out, her blue eyes dancing. "Are you now saying you definitely don't care for him or are you saying you can't quite make up your mind as to how you feel?"

The corners of Skylar's mouth were bracketed with disgust as she sought a plausible explanation of her feelings. "I refuse to be drawn into that trap. As I've already said, he's attractive . . . there's that word again," she began slowly, "in a totally unique manner. Sexy in a way that's completely masculine. He's tall, and his body is in perfect condition. But then," she added cryptically, "I suppose if one in his particular profession doesn't keep in shape, he doesn't last very long, does he? For every redeeming quality, there are just as many minus points."

"Meow . . ." Francine chuckled. "Is he handsome?"

"No. Definitely not handsome. But there's so much strength there, one automatically knows that he would be an awesome adversary."

Her friend leaned back in her chair. "You do realize, of course, that you've just described something between a Greek god and a hero out of a science fiction movie."

"Sorry." Skylar looked flustered, twin dots of color darkening her cheeks. "That's the way I see him."

"How about this wound you say he has?"

"It's nasty looking, but he says, and I agree, that it looks worse than it really is. Unless something completely unforeseen happens, then it should heal without any problems."

Francine took a deep breath. "Everything you've told me sounds like some incredible dream, don't you think?"

"Try living that incredible dream, my dear,

and see how you feel then," Skylar reminded her. "On top of that, he called me at the restaurant this morning and asked if I minded his doing a little cleaning. You can imagine the questions and looks I've been getting from Hubie and Joey. Hearing only one side of a conversation leaves ample room for speculation."

"Knowing how you dislike keeping house, I'm positive you jumped at the chance to get a little free help."

"I didn't object exactly." Skylar frowned. How could she explain that she didn't want Logan Gant touching her things? She simply wanted him to recuperate and get out of her life. Even his name was upsetting to her. "It's just—I'm a very private person, Franny. You know that."

"Mmmm. That may be, honey, but I think you're protesting a little too much where your Mr. Gant is concerned. Offhand, I'd say you're terrified of the man . . . and for all the wrong reasons."

"What's that crack supposed to mean?" Skylar asked sharply.

"Think for a minute, Sky. You're still smarting from your experience with Tim. Along comes this Logan Gant and you immediately see Tim all over again."

"Is that so bad? I mean, Logan *is* involved

in basically the same line of work as Tim was. And judging from his behavior, I'd say he's been with the agency for a number of years. He appears very seasoned in his profession."

"The mystery mounts." Francine grinned. "The minute I get off work, I'm heading straight for your apartment. By the way, does this mean you won't be joining us this evening?"

"Indeed not," Skylar declared, pushing back her chair and standing. "I felt obliged to let him use my guest room, but that's where the obligation stops. I draw the line at entertaining him. Besides, I'm looking forward to being with John . . . and you and Curt too."

In Skylar's neat cream-and-blue kitchen Logan was seated at the table, holding the receiver between shoulder and cheek. One sock-clad foot was propped on the rung of another chair, and there was an expression of distinct annoyance on his face. "And that's all you've been able to find out?" he asked in a disbelieving tone.

"We've got out feelers, we're calling in some markers, we're even relying heavily on double agents," Rainbow replied. "Whatever this is, Hawk, it's big."

"Any inkling yet as to why they kicked off their 'campaign' by trying to wipe out Orka?"

"We have gotten a little bit of information along those lines. Seems they—whoever the hell 'they' are—feel Orka is the most threatening of the usual governmental agencies. Putting two and two together and coming up with five, I, and several others here in the office, feel Achmed's murder, yours and Leighman's accidents, and this clown trailing you, have all been well orchestrated events, aimed at crippling our international covert network."

"In other words, if we're so damned busy defending ourselves, we won't have time to worry about anything else. Right?"

"You got it. However," Rainbow said in a gloating voice that brought the ghost of a smile to Logan's lips, "we just might be on to something."

"Something significant?"

"Perhaps. Give me a few more hours and I'll get back to you. Let's talk about you personally. How are things going? Is the lady cooperating?"

Logan couldn't help but smile at the question, remembering Skylar's reaction to his request that he be allowed to stay in her apartment for a few days. "To a point, and aside from the fact that she hates law enforcement of any description, including all humans involved—especially men—I suppose you could

98

say we're hanging in there. There is one thing. Is there someone available in our office who could keep an eye on her?"

"Twenty-four hours?"

"Yes," Logan said decisively. "If it gets out that she's helping me, she could be in for some real trouble."

"I'll have someone on her before five o'clock. I think Cal Lightfoot. You have any objections?"

"Lightfoot is fine."

"By the way, that info you phoned in this morning, regarding your roomie, has all checked out. Other than being known for demonstrating for various causes and a few parking tickets—which she hasn't paid—she's clean as a whistle. From everything we can find out, she sounds like a very interesting female." Allen chuckled. "I'm looking forward to meeting her."

"So am I," Logan said with a malicious gleam in his eye. "I'd like to see you defending yourself with this fire-eater I'm jailed with."

"It's all in the way you handle them," Allen said smugly."

"I'll remember that, O great one, the very next time I see you floundering like a fish while some cute little blonde makes a

damned fool out of you. I'll call you tomorrow."

Logan replaced the receiver, then leaned
back in his chair. He was relieved Skylar was
exactly who she was supposed to be. It was
also a relief to him to know that the agency
would have someone protecting her as well.
He rubbed at the determined line of his jaw as
he tried to come to terms with the different
emotions this woman stirred within him. One
minute he was ready to strangle her, the next
found him wanting to kiss her. A fool. That's
what he was, he thought derisively, a man
nearly forty years old who could easily make a
fool of himself over a woman in her twenties.

He got up and began restlessly pacing
about the apartment. His hands were clasped
behind his hips, his lips pursed thoughtfully,
as he remembered another time he'd experi-
enced something similar. It'd been how long?
He frowned. How long had it been? Twelve?
Fifteen years?

A key sounded in the lock of the front door
and Logan froze. He stepped into the dark-
ened hall, instinctively angling his body so
that his uninjured side was facing the door
and he had a clear view of whoever was about
to enter the room. The door opened, and Skylar, followed by a tall, striking brunette, entered.

Logan stepped into the living room, his gaze alert as he stared pointedly from the newcomer to Skylar.

"Skylar," he said, "I wasn't aware we were expecting a guest."

Skylar wasn't listening. She was standing in the middle of the room, her stunned gaze darting about crazily. "Am I dreaming, Francine, or has some idiot completely rearranged the furniture in this room?"

CHAPTER SIX

"Er . . . I believe—" Francine began, only to be rudely cut off by Logan.

"Who is your friend, Skylar?" There was a certain wariness in his eyes and an added alertness in the stance of his powerful body.

"Never mind who my friend is, Logan Gant," Skylar began. She marched over to where he was standing, oblivious to the danger signals he was sending out. "What the flaming hell have you done to this room? I'll have you know it took me months to find the perfect piece of furniture for each spot. Now, in less than"—she consulted her watch— "nine hours, you've thrown my entire decorating scheme out the window. Explain yourself, Mr. Gant."

Logan crossed his arms over his wide chest and quietly regarded the small, furious female before him. "I thought we'd dispensed with Ms. and Mr."

"We've dispensed with nothing," she flung

at him. "And don't you dare try to sidetrack me, you toad. I want an explanation this instant!"

Logan shook his head and shrugged his shoulders simultaneously. "It's simple. I thought it needed jazzing up a bit. So"—he gestured expansively with both hands—"I made a few changes."

Skylar stamped her foot in frustration. "Ooooh . . . how dare you stand there and tell me this room needed 'jazzing up'! If left alone, you'd probably have it looking like the parlor of a house of prostitution. It was perfect—just perfect the way it was. When you phoned me this morning, the only thing you asked was permission to do a little cleaning. I didn't give you carte blanche to redo my home."

"I think it looks nice," Logan calmly replied, though he was finding it difficult not to laugh. She was so angry with him, she was actually trembling. And her eyes—why, her eyes were like large green pools. He wondered if they changed color when she was making love?

"It looks hideous," she snapped.

"Why don't you introduce me to your friend," Logan suggested, hoping to change the subject. For more years than he cared to remember, he'd made a habit of not sitting with his back toward doors. He wondered what Skylar would say if he told her that he'd moved the furniture so that the door could be seen from both chairs and the sofa.

She'd probably bash in your head, you dope. She's almost paranoid regarding any changes in her life remotely connected with people who indulge in covert activities— mainly her former fiancé and you.

For a moment Skylar was tempted to tell him to go straight to hell, but common courtesy prevailed. "This is Francine Winter, my best friend and also my neighbor. Francine, I'd like you to meet . . ." she looked to Logan before mentioning his name. Even though at the moment she hated him, she really didn't want to see something happen to another human being because of her carelessness.

"Logan Gant," he quickly supplied, stepping forward and offering Francine his hand.

Skylar glared at her friend as she watched Logan literally charm Francine off her feet. After observing the disgusting display for a few minutes, she decided she'd had enough.

"Have you forgotten we're going out this evening?" she asked Francine. "According to my watch we only have an hour before our dates arrive."

"I apologize for keeping you, Francine," Logan continued in a manner guaranteed to make Skylar lose her lunch in less than five minutes if she were forced to listen much longer to his outrageous line. "Perhaps there'll be another time when we can have coffee together and chat."

"Sounds terrific," Francine agreed—so quickly, Skylar was tempted to reach across the small space between them and smack her! What the hell was the matter with those two? "How about tomorrow?"

"Tomorrow sounds fine. What's your schedule? Do you work from eight to five?"

"Actually"—she smiled—"I'm sort of my own boss. I sell ads for a local television station. My apartment is the third one down from here. Say one o'clock tomorrow afternoon?"

"Tomorrow at one. Shall I bring dessert?"

"Oh, please!" Skylar exclaimed, darting glaring looks from friend to roomie. "Spare me. I wish you could hear yourselves. You sound like Betty Crocker and the Welcome Wagon representative." She turned with a disgusted toss of her head and stormed from the room.

Damnation! she silently yelled as she entered her bedroom and slammed the door. The events of the past twenty-four hours were beginning to stretch her nerves to the breaking point. She'd had a lousy day at the restaurant, knowing she had a spy in her apartment hadn't helped her peace of mind, and then she'd come home to find he'd re-arranged her living room. Now, to add insult to injury, he was attempting to charm her best friend and neighbor.

She caught a glimpse of her face in the mirror and paused, staring at her stormy features. Slowly, hesitantly, she moved closer to the dresser, raising one hand to her face, her fingertips lightly, hesitantly, touching her cheek as the snowballing flight of her thoughts was quietly brought under control.

What was there about Logan Gant that annoyed her so badly? she asked her worried reflection . . . aside from the fact that he'd literally pushed his way into her life. She certainly wasn't afraid of the man. In fact, she grudgingly mused, she really believed his incredible story, else she would never have agreed to let him stay.

Why not face the truth? the more practical, critical side of her suggested. You've already admitted to yourself and to Francine that he's a very sexy man. Add sexy to the air of mystery surrounding him, and you have the perfect male every woman is supposed to be looking for. Can it be that you're afraid of what the mystery will reveal?

Afraid? Skylar tried mentally to shrug off the suggestion.

Of course. You were hurt very much by Tim, and what you consider his 'betrayal' of your relationship because of his devotion to his work. To allow yourself to become even remotely interested in a man like Logan Gant would constitute an unforgivable sin in your eyes.

That's ridiculous.

But even as she went through the automatic motions of quietly denying the accusation, she was left with an uneasy feeling. A feeling one encountered when one knew something was terribly wrong, but was unable to put one's finger directly on the problem.

Finally tiring of playing the futile game of self-analysis, she undressed and started toward the door to the bathroom. Suddenly she stopped, wheeled about, and made a mad dash for her closet and her robe. All she needed to get things really sizzling between herself and Logan Gant was to go parading around naked in front of the damned man.

Shower, makeup, and dressing were handled in record time. With a good twenty minutes to spare before her date arrived, Skylar left her room with a determined gleam in her eyes. There were a few ground rules that needed to be established if there was to be any kind of harmony between her and Logan Gant. She was also curious about the agency he worked for and the reason behind his near assassination.

She found him in the kitchen, humming while he went about preparing his dinner. "We have to talk," she announced from the doorway. It was unbelievable, she thought peevishly. He was acting as if he weren't hiding out, but on holiday. Just looking at him, one would never guess he was a glorified G-man.

Logan turned from his preoccupation with a steak, his deep blue eyes floating over her like a sudden caress. A burst of need tightened into a knot of desire in his gut as he studied Skylar. The green dress she wore matched the color of her eyes, intensifying their brilliance, drawing Logan inevitably to the slender flame of her body. "Something bothering you, Skylar?"

"You *could* say that," she replied archly. "I think it should be understood from this point on, that you will—er—refrain . . . from making any additional changes in my home. I worked very hard on the room you destroyed today."

"I don't like sitting with my back to a door."

"I don't care where you sit, Logan, just as long as you leave my apartment intact."

"Every chair in your living room, and the sofa, were at such an angle that the person sitting in them had his or her back to the door at all times."

Skylar looked totally confused. "So?"

"In my particular line of work, Skylar, only fools sit with their backsides unguarded."

"You mean . . ." her eyes grew round with horrified comprehension.

"Precisely."

"But I thought you said no one knew you were here."

"They don't. I managed to lose them, or I would never have come here. However, if they're the experts we think them to be, they'll find a way to get a list of all the passengers on the plane. You'd be checked out by them whether or not you'd ever seen me. As a matter of fact, I . . ." he paused. Some inner voice of caution kept him from revealing to her that an Orka agent was her constant shadow. At the moment he felt the revelation would only serve to upset her more.

"Yes?" Skylar prodded.

"I was thinking of changing around my bedroom tomorrow, but I suppose it can wait."

"You are not to touch another piece of my

furniture," she said in a low, threatening voice. Though to be honest, she knew she was more frightened than mad.

Logan appeared properly chastened, and for a moment Skylar was almost tempted to laugh at the woebegone expression. "I'll stick to cleaning and cooking," he countered in true martyred fashion. "Any objections to those two things, or do you have some special reason why I shouldn't do either?"

Skylar waved one trembling hand. "Be my guest."

Logan watched her closely, seeing the tiny fissures of fear spreading over her, her shaking hand, and her attempt to cover it. "Is there something else bothering you?"

"Why are you being chased, and what is the name of the organization with which you're associated?" She'd hoped to couch the questions with a bit more finesse, but the overwrought state of her emotions hadn't let her. Somehow or other, Aunt Katherine had failed to teach her how to handle people being shot and baldheaded men bursting through her front door.

Logan looked down at the steak. He even nudged it into a different position with the tip of one finger, then licked the taste of the marinade from his skin with his tongue. Stalling for time seemed dumb, he decided. On the other hand—if it were to become known that Skylar was helping him . . . "What brought that up?" He looked back at her then, his gaze as revealing as a granite wall.

And though Skylar certainly was a babe compared to Logan when it came to assessing people, even she saw the mask slip into place. "Well, you must admit it's a legitimate question."

"But why now . . . at this precise moment? Has something happened today that you aren't telling me?"

"Not unless you were responsible for our chef at Hubie's failing to show up this morning," she retorted with suspect politeness. "However, putting that small, insignificant matter aside, if you want specifics"—she held up her fingers and began ticking off offense after offense—"how about your conduct on the plane . . . the way you burst in here last night . . . the wound in your side, your little foray into interior design." She gave a brittle smile. "Trust me, Logan, when I tell you that it's been at least three days since I helped one of my friends treat his bullet wound, then let him hide out in my apartment."

A crooked grin tugged at one corner of his mouth as he walked over and sat down across from her. He leaned forward, braced his muscled forearms on the edge of the table, and clasped his hands before him. She had spirit, and he liked that . . . even worse, he liked her, and that could only mean pain for both of them. "You don't pull your punches, do you, Ms. Dennis?"

"Not this evening, Mr. Gant, and probably not tomorrow either." Before she could elaborate, the phone rang.

Logan plucked the receiver from its cradle with one large hand and passed it across to her. "Hello?"

"Skylar? Is that you?"

"Yes, Mrs. D. How are you?"

"Fine, dear, but I've been waiting for you to call me."

"I apologize, Mrs. D. Things were so hectic at the restaurant today, I lost track of time. When I did get a chance to give you a ring, you didn't answer. I wanted to see if I could bring Tim's medal around tomorrow?"

"Did everything go well?"

"Everything went very smoothly. His captain said some very nice things about Tim. You would have been thrilled. I have everything on tape for you. There was a time or two when I tried to explain that I was only accepting the medal in your place, but no one listened. They kept referring to me as Tim's fiancée. I hope you understand in the event someone should mention that to you."

113

"How can you even think of such a thing!" Mrs. Dawson exclaimed. "You went as a personal favor to me, and I do appreciate it. So, I'm sure, does Tim. I'm positive that at this very moment, he's looking down at you with a huge smile of gratitude on his face."

"I'm not so sure about that, Mrs. D." Unconsciously, Skylar glanced toward the ceiling. Feeling she had known Tim a little better than his mother had, she wouldn't have been at all surprised to see her former fiancé scowling down at her, with some remark such as "God! Only you can get things so screwed up, Sky."

"Of course he would. I know my Tim, and he had the good sense to pick you, so that settles the matter. By the way, I'm going out this evening, why don't I just stop by your place and pick up the medal and the tape?"

"Actually," Skylar said quickly, turning two shades paler at the mere thought of Mrs. Dawson coming face to face with Logan Gant, "I'm also going out. In fact, I'm already dressed. My date should be here any minute."

"Oh? Now that's something my Timmie definitely wouldn't like—you seeing other men. I really do hate to see you replace him so quickly in your life, dear. It's only been six months and three days."

An angry glint entered Skylar's eyes. "Mrs.

D., are you forgetting that I broke up with Tim three weeks before he died? This isn't the first date I've had since we quit seeing each other."

The older woman made a loud noise of exhaling. "I'm sure you know best, dear. I'll look for you around ten-thirty in the morning."

"Ten-thirty sounds great. See you then."

She practically threw the receiver at Logan, then began drumming the tips of her fingers against the table. "Why do some people refuse to accept the hard, cold facts of life? I mean ,. . . Tim's dead! He has been dead for six months. Where does his mother get off trying to make me feel like a monster because I'm going out to dinner and the theater?"

"Would I be correct in assuming the person with whom you were just speaking is your former fiancé's mother?" Logan asked politely.

"You assume correctly. I went to Houston expressly as a favor to Tim's mother. He was awarded a posthumous honor at a banquet. His mother refused to go and accept the award. She called and begged me to go in her stead, and I did." Skylar looked steadily at Logan. "That's why I had the misfortune to be on the plane you boarded. Needless to say, I didn't enjoy my stay in that city nor the return trip."

"Sorry," Logan felt compelled to say. "I take it Mrs. D. isn't too happy with you seeing other men?"

"Aren't you being a bit personal?"

"You did bring up the question."

Skylar sighed. "So I did. To answer your question, yes . . . she's very annoyed. She still hasn't accepted the fact that Tim and I had broken up a few weeks before his death."

"She sounds like a very determined woman."

"More of an airhead, actually. I'm her one remaining link with Tim, so I suppose until her grief and acceptance of his death is an accomplished fact, she'll continue to regard me as an extension of her son. Annoying, but quite harmless and very pathetic. She can be irritating, but I feel sorry for her."

Logan was quiet for several moments. "You're a very compassionate woman," he said, luxuriating in her scented presence and enjoying the aura of contentment wafting from her. She was one of those rare individuals who really cared for other people. "You made a trip that had to be unpleasant at best for you, all because an older woman asked you to. You helped me when you thought I was in trouble on the plane, and later, you took me into your home. Exactly who do you go to for shoring up, Skylar Dennis?"

It was a question she'd never been asked, one she didn't have an answer for. A hint of color added its glow to her cheeks. "I—I suppose I've always managed to manage on my own."

"Last night, when you first opened the door to me, you thought I'd brought bad news about someone named Katherine? Is she a relative of yours?"

"My aunt." Skylar smiled. "She's crusty and something of an eccentric, but I adore her. She raised me. What about you, Logan. Where are you from? Are your parents living?"

"If this is to be an exchange of confidences," he said, smiling expansively, "why don't we make it more pleasurable by sharing a cup of coffee, mmmmm?"

"A quick one," Skylar agreed, feeling pleased as punch that she was finally going to learn something about the man presently occupying her guest bedroom. She sat back and watched him, marveling at how easily he'd made himself at home in her home. To an innocent bystander it had to look as if they were living together, happy as larks.

"Will you be able to soothe Mrs. D.'s ruffled feelings when you see her tomorrow?" Logan asked as he poured coffee into two chocolate-brown mugs and brought them over to the table.

"I'll certainly try. But if she won't listen, then I'm afraid she'll have to adapt. I refuse to allow Tim—through his mother—to dominate my life from the grave. I've decided from now on, that instead of bottling up my feelings and renewing my ulcer every six months, I'm going to be more assertive with people."

"Since I happen to know I'm the latest culprit to annoy you, I hope you'll accept my apology." How he was managing to keep a straight face, Logan wasn't sure. But he knew if he laughed, the green-eyed vixen seated across the table from him was likely to part his skull with a baseball bat.

"There's no doubt about it, you've done your share," Skylar readily agreed. He had the most interesting face she'd ever seen.

Must you keep on repeating yourself? the tiny voice inside her asked. You keep telling Francine that, and you keep telling yourself that. For Pete's sake, come up with something new. I'm tired of hearing the same old thing over and over. And just between you and me, I don't find his face interesting at all.

Well, he is interesting, Skylar continued the silent argument. He wasn't handsome, he was involved in heaven only knew what, he'd

118

been shot, and he was an admitted spy. If that wasn't interesting, she'd like to know what was. "Unfortunately, my week had already started downhill before I had the dubious honor of being singled out by you."

"Ahh, yes. Tim's medal?" he asked curiously. "Care to cry on my shoulder?—metaphorically speaking, of course," he hastened to add. Privately, he had a feeling that Skylar Dennis, petite thought she may have been, wasn't one to cry on anyone's shoulder. What was it Allen had said: she was involved in all sorts of "Save the—" movements? Funny, Logan mused, for whatever reason fate had had for sending Skylar Dennis his way, he found to his amazement that he enjoyed her company immensely. He wanted to know everything there was about her—from her friends down to her favorite scent, what foods she liked best . . . her favorite flowers . . . colors . . .

"How would you like to be seated at the head table in a huge banquet hall and be the focal point of every eye in the room?"

"Sounds terrifying."

"It was."

"If Tim hadn't already been dead, I can promise you, I would have killed him the minute I set eyes on him."

119

"I can certainly understand your reasoning," Logan replied solemnly.

Skylar tipped her head to one side, a grin of amusement curving her inviting lips. "Know something, Logan Gant?"

He sat forward, his broad shoulders hunched, his huge hands clasped around the hot mug of coffee. Her smile was infectious, and Logan felt as if he'd had just been run over by a very long freight train. "You tell me, Skylar Dennis," he said huskily.

"You are a very easy person to talk to. How is it that some woman hasn't snatched you up before now and taken you away from that infernal 'agency' you appear wedded to?"

Logan reached across the table, his forefinger tracing the outline of her lips and feeling the moisture still on them from her last sip of coffee. They were firm and soft and hot—three textures in one . . . distinct, yet each of them one third of the whole. He left the mouth and cupped her cheek, allowing his palm to mold to the shape of fragile bone and soft, fragrant skin. Never in his life before had he been so turned on by the simple touching of another person.

Skylar stared into blue eyes burning into hers, eyes that were as warm and inviting now as they had been cold and unreadable moments ago. The contrast was stunning. His hand on her face turned an awareness of feeling heretofore unknown to her into an acute longing for something more. It was as if each and every sense she possessed was intensified, each strained to its very limits and beyond to savor the moment and absorb the impact.

She saw Logan slowly rise to his feet. Without stopping to think Skylar followed the lead of his hand. She was small and petite, her auburn hair gleaming like burnished copper. Gentle but firm, he urged her upward with his hand, her green dress shimmering in the light like liquid emeralds as it set itself against her slender figure.

He drew her into his arms and she went willingly. His mouth took command in a kiss that had her grasping his shoulders for support. His lips touched hers quickly, his tongue delving deeply into her mouth only to retract and taste the fullness of her lips. He paid homage to her eyes, her cheeks, her forehead, the sensitive tips of her ears. Kissing, caressing, learning every angle and inch of that part of her and committing it to memory.

At some later date, when he would no longer be in need of Skylar Dennis's help and would be sitting in some dimly lit bar in God knows where, Logan knew he would pull from his memory the image of Skylar in his arms and the feel of her parted lips beneath his, and the short, raspy breaths she drew as if she'd only just completed a marathon.

The doorbell sounded.

Logan silently damned whoever it was whose finger was pressing the tiny black button.

A quiver of surprise jerked through his tall body, drawing him to his full height. He raised his head and rested his chin on Skylar's hair. "I think your date has arrived, Ms. Dennis," he murmured softly.

"So he has, Mr. Gant, so he has. Offhand I'd say his timing is lousy. Under the circumstance, however, I'd venture to say he's saved me from a very painful experience, wouldn't you?"

"Painful, Ms. Dennis?" Logan smiled tenderly. Two long fingers kept her head immobile while he studied her. "How can you say the experience is painful when you've never tried it?"

"Once was enough."

"You were dealing with a young boy masquerading as an adult, honey."

"Are you implying it would be different with you?"

"Implying?" he rasped huskily. "A man never implies when the subject is of such grave importance. I know it would be different." He dropped a feathery kiss on her forehead, then placed his hands on her shoulders and gently urged her toward the door. "Go. Have dinner, go to the theater, enjoy dancing or whatever it is you plan to do this evening with your young man."

But Skylar wasn't to be put off so easily. She turned and looked up at him, expressions of sadness and triumph warring for a place of prominence in her gaze. "Why, Logan Gant," she murmured in a barely audible voice. "You're as big a coward as I am, aren't you?"

CHAPTER SEVEN

Dinner with John, Francine, and Curt was pleasant enough, but Skylar found it next to impossible to keep her mind off Logan. His kisses—and her responses to them—were something she was going to have to deal with sooner or later. Even Tim, the man she'd thought she loved, and whom she had agreed to marry, hadn't drawn the same breathless responses from her that Logan's lovemaking did. What he'd said to her earlier came to mind. In retrospect Tim did seem like a teenager compared to Logan. Though their professions might possibly be similar, Skylar now realized the two men were totally different.

Her thoughts were uncontrollable as a pogo stick as they bounced from incident to incident. She was midway through dinner, however, when it dawned on her that she hadn't gleaned a single bit of information from Logan regarding his personal life. Every question she'd posed, he'd neatly sidestepped . . .

every single one. His quest into her private life, however, hadn't been nearly so unfruitful, she frowned. Why, she'd been like the veritable fountain of information, babbling like crazy in response to every question he asked.

"Something bothering you?" Francine asked later as they freshened their makeup in the ladies' room before going on to the theater. She'd been aware of her friend's steadily declining mood for some time now and was curious. "Did John say something to annoy you?"

Skylar sighed. "Have you ever known John to be anything but a perfect gentleman?" She leaned closer to the mirror and touched up her blush. "I'm afraid I'm rather preoccupied with my houseguest this evening."

"Ahh, yes." Francine grinned, watching Skylar out of the corner of her eye. "I'm really looking forward to having a chance to talk with him. He's very friendly, isn't he?"

"Yes . . . well . . . it might not be such a good idea to become so chummy with the man."

"Probably makes about as much sense as you allowing him to stay in your apartment."

"Well." Skylar looked peeved. "If you want to put it that way," she said stiffly.

"Would you rather I not see Logan?"

126

Francine asked, carefully masking her surprise. A jealous Skylar was indeed something new. This was getting more interesting by the second.

"Certainly not," she was hastily assured. "The man means nothing to me other than as a rather unusual and annoying guest. I can only hope my apartment will survive his boredom and confinement."

Francine refrained from commenting. But the more she thought about the situation, the more concerned she became for Skylar's happiness. One look at Logan Gant had left Francine with the impression of strength and determination, of a man immovable once he made up his mind. . . . That was good, Skylar needed his strength. He also appeared to be of an age when changing professions was out of the question. . . . That wasn't so good. Skylar detested the "profession" in question. That being the case, Francine realized her chances of playing matchmaker were defeated before she even started.

The evening wore on for Skylar with the boring regularity of a dull toothache. She smiled at the proper times in response to John's humorous quips, listened attentively to the funny stories told by Curt, Francine's date. But throughout each word and gesture, she was all but physically removed from the laughing foursome.

By the time John left her at her door, Skylar felt emotionally drained.

"How about going to the Saints game with me on Sunday?" he asked after a brief kiss that left Skylar as unmoved as a concrete block.

"Fine," she replied, then, minutes later as she was unlocking her door, wondered why on earth she'd agreed. She didn't pursue the answer; her eyes and her thoughts were too busy looking for Logan.

Don't be so silly, she scolded herself. Did you really expect the man to be waiting up for you?

Unconsciously her shoulders straightened and her chin tilted upward a fraction of an inch while she bounced back from the frank ridicule. Could she help it if she was anxious for the darn man?

And just who do you expect to believe such a preposterous lie?

The question went unanswered, however, when it became evident to Skylar that Logan was either gone or asleep. She dropped her small clutch purse and wrap onto the sofa, stepped out of her heels, then walked down the hall to the door of his room. It was slightly ajar and she didn't hesitate to push it open farther in order to see better.

"I was beginning to think you were going to spend the night with your friend," the deep voice sounded in the near darkness, causing Skylar to jump at least a foot off the floor.

"Must you be so quiet and underhanded about every damned thing you do?" she shot at him when she was able to speak again.

"My, my, Ms. Dennis. What happened? Did your date prove lacking?"

She walked on over to the edge of the bed, her arms crossed at her waist, and peered down at him. "Exactly what does that crack mean?"

"I should think a pretty young woman like you would come in from a date singing. You should be happy . . . floating on air. As it is, you have a distinct frown on your face, and you are grouchy as a bear. Why?"

"None of your business," she snapped. "Why are you lying on the bed in your clothes?"

"Is that another of the no-nos in your household? Is one required to disrobe completely in order to take a short snooze?"

"Don't be more of an ass than you already are, Gant. I'm in no mood for your bad humor. I simply thought you weren't feeling well or something. Now that I see there's nothing to my fears, I'll leave you alone." She turned to leave, but Logan caught her hand. Before she could jerk it away, he pulled her down beside him on the bed.

"Don't go just yet," he murmured gruffly.

Skylar squinted in an attempt to catch a better look at his face. Was there something he wasn't telling her? Had someone tried to force his way into the apartment? She knew he'd gone out that morning, though she hadn't mentioned it to him. She'd known because of his steak. There were rib eyes in the fridge; he'd been marinating a New York strip. Had he pushed his luck and gone out the second time and had another run-in with his friend? Had he been shot again?

She reached down and gripped his shoulders, her fear enabling her to shake him a bit —in spite of his size. "Logan?" There was panic in her voice as her fertile thoughts jelled into one huge, overriding fear that he quite possibly was ill and about to die.

"No, honey," he corrected her in a firm, gentle fashion. "I'm not going to die—at least not at the moment, and not for a very long time . . . I hope. However, if you keep shaking me, I can't promise you much." He caught her hands in his and brought them down to rest against his chest. His shirt was open, and Skylar couldn't believe how beautifully excit-

130

ing it was to feel the silky coarseness of dark hair beneath her fingertips. "What's wrong? Why are you so upset?"

"Y-you're what's wrong," she stormed at him, her emotions still running along a very narrow, jagged edge. Her voice trailed off to a mere whisper and Logan had to strain to hear her. "I was . . . I still am . . . afraid for you. When you weren't in the living room or the kitchen I thought you had gone out again and been injured . . . or that you'd been killed."

"Would it really matter to you, Skylar, if something did happen to me?"

"Of course it would, you stupid ox!" She pushed back, becoming embarrassed by her outburst and her increasing awareness of Logan the man as opposed to Logan the spy. "I would hate to see anyone hurt or killed."

"Ahh, yes, we mustn't forget Ms. Dennis, the servant of the public. Your concern is only for me as a human being, not as someone special to you. Correct?" He was deliberately goading her, Logan told himself, but for some indefinable reason he couldn't stop. On top of everything else, he'd spent a miserable evening thinking of her with another man.

That's selfish as hell, a small voice whispered. Besides, you weren't exactly invited into her home, remember? She has a life and friends that you know nothing about. You'd do well to recognize that fact and not try your damndest to become a large part of her past. For that is what you will be, you know—her past.

"If you'll excuse me," Skylar said quietly, "I have a headache. I think I'll go to bed." She stood, then glanced down at him. "I'm glad you're all right."

"I'm afraid I have to disagree with you on that score, honey."

"What are you talking about?"

"Remember last night when you wanted me to see a doctor?" She nodded. "Well, I should have listened to you. Since around noon today, my side has been bothering me quite a bit. I've been keeping a close check on it, and it's beginning to look really inflamed."

Without thinking, Skylar sat on the edge of the bed, then reached for the lamp and clicked it on. Logan threw a hand over his eyes in a reflexive gesture. "Was that necessary?" he asked in a roaring voice.

"Would you prefer me to try to check the wound by braille?" she challenged him, all the while pushing aside the unrestricting material of his shirt and baring his side. She lifted the edge of the loose edge of the bandage, then gasped.

"Dear heavens!" she murmured the moment she was able to get a good look. "This is terrible." Stern green eyes met pain-filled blue ones. "Will you please tell me why you thought you had to be so closed mouthed?"

"I'm accustomed to living my life in a very closed-mouthed atmosphere, Ms. Dennis," he reminded her in a short, clipped tone. "I see no reason to change."

"I'll give you several good reasons, Mr. Gant," she hissed angrily. "*You* took it upon yourself to invade *my* space on the airplane. *You* saw fit to come crawling to *me* for help when some lowlife tried to blow you away. And *you* have been making yourself at home in *my* apartment, sleeping in one of *my* beds, eating *my* food, et cetera. In the words of a very old song, Mr. Gant, 'I've grown accustomed to your face.' Need I continue?"

Logan's lips, sensuous and inviting to Skylar even in her anger, twitched humorously. "Point taken, Ms. Dennis."

"Great! Now, get off your behind and onto your sizable feet, Mr. Gant. Do you know that your feet were one of the first things I noticed about you? They're huge, and those awful sandals were terrible. Oh, well, that's not important at the moment. We're going to the hospital, and I suspect we need to do a bit of organizing before we attempt the trip. Correct?"

A grudging respect shone in Logan's dulled

gaze. "If you ever decide to change directions in your life, let me know. My agency can always use a woman who has courage and a sharp mind."

"I'd rather eat bread and water for the rest of my life than become a member of a group of people I completely detest. Can you manage by yourself while I call Francine?"

Logan frowned. "I'm having a difficult enough time worrying about involving you; why bring Francine into it?"

"Because she is a member of a little theater group and has a couple of large boxes of makeup and wigs and all sorts of goodies."

A suspicious look washed over his face. Skylar grinned. He looked more afraid of her hand at disguising him than he did of the prospect of going to the hospital. "May I ask exactly who it is you will be escorting to the hospital?"

"Why . . . my dear Aunt Katherine, of course."

"Will you please stop messing with the controls?" Skylar snapped for the second or third time in a very short span of time. She pushed a straggling strand of hair back beneath the knitted cap she was wearing. "You are driving me up the wall."

"Well, let me be the first to inform you, Ms.

Dennis, up the wall would be a hell of a lot better than where you are about to drive me, and that's off this damned balcony!" Logan practically screamed.

Francine rushed forward to grab one side of the wheelchair, and Skylar got the other one. Between them they grunted and struggled till it was aimed at the exit, and not directly toward the three-foot drop-off and ultimately the pool.

"Just stay cool and calm, 'Aunt Katherine.' " Francine patted the arm of the "old lady" consolingly. "It won't be long now before you'll be seeing your dear Dr. Weston. He'll give you something for that terrible ole tummy ache, and you'll be all better."

Logan regarded the bearer of those words of "comfort" with the same degree of cordiality he would a viper. "You sound like an idiot," he whispered hoarsely.

"You're an ungrateful pig," Francine whispered right back. "I hope you get a four-inch needle stuck in your behind."

"Thanks!"

"Anytime."

"Er . . . girls," "Aunt Katherine" twittered in a tone of voice strangely modulated between a frog's croak and the simpering tone of an Edwardian dandy, "let's do be a bit more quick, shall we? We need less conversa-

135

tion and more action. You young people today . . . I'm feeling positively faint from all the excitement."

"I'd be delighted to hurry, Auntie dear," Skylar told him in a saccharine-sweet voice. "Just say the word and I'll let you have a little midnight swim."

"Ha!" "Aunt Katherine" snorted in a raucous undertone. "Just get your skinny little butt into overdrive, honey. All this garb the two of you've got me stuffed into is itching me to death, not to mention this wig you've got skewered to my scalp. I feel like I've been captured and scalped by the Comanches."

"That's exactly what that baldheaded ass would like to do if he could catch you," Skylar threw at him without a hint of kindness. "He'd gladly give you to the Comanches—if they were still in business, and if they would let him watch them torture you. On the other hand, I happen to be one-eighth Indian, and I resent having my heritage besmirched by even thinking of comparing them to the idiot chasing you."

When the warring trio reached the small, battered car, it became a three-ringed circus as Skylar and Francine tried to assist "Aunt Katherine" into the front seat. At the completion of the effort, both girls looked at each other and exhaled loudly.

136

"I am delighted he's your guest. I take back every nice thing I said about him," Francine told her friend. "He is a royal pain in the behind."

"Hear that, Auntie dear?" Skylar bent down and looked at Logan through the window on the passenger side. "My neighbor here thinks you're a pain in the behind. How does that grab you, you old bat?"

"Are you sure you don't want me to go with you?" Francine asked.

"I'm positive. You stay here in case I have to call you. Dr. Weston is to meet Logan at the hospital in forty-five minutes."

"This is the wildest scheme I've ever heard of. Do you really think it will work?"

Logan's voice joined in the conversation. "It'll work. That is, if we ever get the show on the road." He glared up at the two women, then dropped his head back against the seat.

Skylar opened the passenger door and retrieved a portion of the hem of his dress and tossed it on his lap. "Hang on to that so it won't get caught in the door again, or I just might scalp you myself."

"Yes, ma'am." Logan scowled, his eyes never leaving her as she and Francine maneuvered the collapsible wheelchair into the trunk of the VW. Skylar walked on around to the passenger side and slid into the driver's

137

seat, while Francine put thumb and forefinger-tips together in a gesture of A-okay, then turned and went back inside the apartment complex. "Won't this damned seat go back any farther? I feel like my legs are being jammed into my spine."

"Be content that they're just jamming into your spine. I can think of another excellent spot for them to be lodged," Skylar told him. "Now, please stop your carping. My vehicle is extremely temperamental, and I don't need the likes of you sitting beside me going on and on like a bad-tempered little boy."

She placed her foot on the gas pedal and pumped for dear life. While her foot was flying up and down like a dog scratching at fleas, she turned the key in the ignition and the engine sprang to life. She raced the motor, causing the frame of the little car to shimmy and shake as if it were having some mysterious attack.

"Judas Priest!" Logan's eyes became blue circles of disbelief. "You honestly expect me to ride in this?"

"Watch it, buster," he was told unceremoniously as the VW was slammed into reverse. It shot out of the parking slot, then sprang forward like a rock flying out of a slingshot. When the taillights rounded the corner and faded from sight, only the sound of the groaning motor could be heard for a second more, and then it, too, was gone and the usual night sounds prevailed.

From the shadows of a large oak, under which a rather fancy van was parked, a man could be seen emerging. He was of medium height, had ebony-black hair, and a face as unreadable as stone. He'd been witness to the unbelievably funny scene only moments before. In all his years with the agency he'd never seen anything quite as funny as Logan dressed up like a woman. The story would lighten many an evening's conversation in the months to come.

Cal Lightfoot stood staring at the still-lighted windows of Skylar's apartment, and those of her friend, Francine Winter, trying to reach a decision on the best course of action. Suddenly he moved toward the van, opened the door, and got behind the wheel.

He'd been assigned to watch Skylar Dennis, hadn't he? In seconds he was out of the parking lot. It took only a moment or two for him to pick out the taillights of the VW and settle in behind it.

When the little red car reached a certain point on a one-way side street just off Canal Boulevard, the driver found a parking place and stopped. Both occupants of the car got out and walked around the corner onto Canal, where they hailed a taxi.

Skylar gave the name of the hospital, then turned her attention to a very pale Logan. The effort of removing his disguise had left him almost shaking.

"How are you feeling?" she whispered. His forehead was beaded with perspiration and his skin felt clammy when she placed her palm against the side of his face. During the ride he'd calmed down somewhat, and she'd had time to regret a lot of the hateful things she'd hurled at him. It wasn't that she hated him, it just seemed the entire time they'd been together there'd been one major crisis after another.

"Afraid I'll die, Skylar?" he managed the barb in spite of the hot, searing pain in his side.

"Don't tease, Logan." She didn't ask permission, nor did she even consider what she was doing. She simply acted—by moving as close as possible to him and resting her head against his chest, one arm lying across his thighs.

The sharp intake of Logan's breath was lost to Skylar, the sounds of the city and the traffic drowning it out. With the arm on his uninjured side Logan cradled the slimness of her body to him, luxuriating in even that brief

140

instant of oneness and the few moments fate had seen fit to grant him. He rested his chin against the wool cap covering her hair. It had been a long time since he'd felt like this holding a woman. Too damned long. His gaze became faraway as memories flooded his mind.

Memories. Memories that had served him well. They'd carried him through untold lonely hours. They'd warmed his heart on Christmases past and they'd kept him from being alone when others were being welcomed by their loved ones and families.

A fleeting sense of guilt became mingled with the other emotion attempting to push itself to its wobbly legs and take control of his heart. Did he have the right? Dare he push old, trusted, and true memories aside for a chance, even a brief glimpse, of another taste of happiness—a happiness so bright and brilliant it warmed his entire being? There was a tiny smoldering flame on every part of him that was touching her. A flame that only her beauty and her softness could assuage.

Dare he forget his beautiful Iseult and grasp this new love?

CHAPTER EIGHT

"In addition to the prescription for the antibiotic, Mr. Gant, I'm also going to include something that will help you rest."

"That won't be necessary, doctor."

"Nonsense. Though it's not necessarily a deep wound, it's a rough one. All that probing I did, and that small piece of the bullet we found, is going to make it throb like crazy." The doctor consulted his watch. "Since it's as late as it is, I'll have someone take these to the hospital pharmacy and get them filled for you."

"I'd appreciate that." Frankly, Logan was anxious to be on his way. So far, nothing had happened, but that didn't mean it couldn't or that it wouldn't. Terrorists weren't exactly known for respecting other people's lives or property. To the staff and patients of the hospital, he was like a ticking bomb. The sooner he got his business settled and left, the safer they would all be.

By the time the orderly returned to the small cubicle with the prescriptions, Logan's body was bathed in a film of perspiration from the simple chore of calling Skylar and telling her that he was ready. He was weak as a kitten, and his knees were decidedly wobbly.

The orderly watched the big man struggle to his feet and hold on to the metal examining table with both hands as he got his bearings. "Are you sure you're okay, sir?" the young man asked.

"Don't worry, I'll rest a few minutes while I'm waiting to be picked up."

"That's good," the orderly said. "You don't look too good at the moment. If you need anything, just shout."

"Fine." Logan nodded curtly. He took a deep breath, then willed his body to obey him. If the bastards looking for him had the hospitals staked out, they would spot him the minute he stepped outside the building. That being the case, he knew damned well he wasn't going out of this world with both hands clutching the wall in an effort to stay upright.

After waiting fifteen minutes to the second, he began making his way determinedly through the doors of the emergency entrance and to the street. He'd never felt less prepared for battle in his entire life. However, two very important things spurred him on.

One was that Skylar, in accordance with the plan they'd worked out, would already have sent a taxi for him. The other was the safety of the people in the hospital.

No sooner did that thought run through his mind than he saw a taxi barreling toward him. And even though he was expecting to see such a vehicle, he nevertheless braced himself, instinct taking over when physical effort was weak. There sure as hell was more than one taxi in the city of New Orleans. As he watched and waited through those tense seconds, Logan was reminded of a reel of film being shown in slow motion. Everything took on the look and sound of unreality. The taxi slowing to a crawl, his body—bit by bit—pulling itself together for impact. . . .

He'd faced the same situation a number of times during his years with Orka. Yet it never ceased to amaze him how really calm he became when he realized he was quite probably living his last few seconds of life. And in spite of the pain he was in at the moment, that same, peculiar calm passed over him—slipping from his head downward, to slowly envelop each and every inch of him, leaving him with an almost floating sensation. It was eerie . . . unreal.

He was facing death.

His mind, his senses, reeled against such an

admission, yet his body remained steady. What would it be? A gun? A bomb?

Would it be instantaneous or lingering?

The taxi slammed to a stop directly in front of him and the door swung open. "Get your tush in this taxi, Gant, and be quick about it," Skylar said quickly. She was still dressed in her "cat burglar" outfit, her head entirely covered by the dark wool cap. As she was speaking, she was catching hold of him and drawing him inside. When the door was closed, she nodded to the driver, who took off like a bat out of hell.

"Must be a personal friend of yours." Logan grinned crookedly at her as he slumped, relieved, against the seat. "The two of you drive exactly alike."

"Be glad that he does, Logan. Your friend from the plane is in a black sedan, two cars back. Your theory that they would be watching the hospitals was correct."

The cold hand of fear caught Logan in its grip.

Always before he'd been responsible only for himself; or at least, if there had been others, he hadn't known them or seen their faces. But this time was different. For the first time in years he was coming to care for someone, and that very special someone was now in danger of having her life snuffed out—and all because of him.

"Are you sure it was the same man?" he asked Skylar.

"Do you honestly think anyone could see that face and head and forget?" She laughed nervously. "What do we do now?"

Logan reached down to the half-boots he was wearing, pulled up the right trouser leg, and removed a small pistol. He passed the weapon to an inside pocket of the navy blazer, then looked at an ashen-faced Skylar. "Useless as hell at the moment, but nonetheless comforting."

He turned with his back toward the door, enabling him to see behind the taxi. A dark sedan, such as the one Skylar had mentioned, was two or three cars behind them and constantly attempting to pass the cars ahead and move up closer to the taxi.

So intent was the driver of the sedan on gaining on the taxi, he paid little attention to the flashy blue-and-cream van that had pulled alongside and was steadily inching toward the driver's side of the sedan.

Logan, who was watching the traffic, saw what was happening. At first he thought the driver of the van to be slightly intoxicated. But the longer he watched, the more convinced he became that only an individual with an absolutely clear mind could keep his vehicle under such tight control without crashing.

When the man driving the sedan realized he was about to be made sandwich filling between a van and a garbage truck, he panicked. Logan saw the car swerve to the right, smack against the heavy truck. The van shot forward just as the car swerved to the left . . . and slammed into the broadside of another vehicle, a light-colored car.

Another automobile joined the fray—one with a set of revolving lights on top. All three vehicles—garbage truck, dark sedan, and light-colored car—were halted. The last thing Logan saw was the baldheaded man bursting out of the car, gesturing wildly.

Skylar, who had also been a witness to the erratic driving habits of the threesome, turned to the man seated beside her. "That was close."

"Too damned close," Logan muttered gruffly. Without another word he reached for her, pulling her close to his chest, their hearts beating crazily.

"The driver of that van must know you folks," the taxi driver spoke over his shoulder.

Logan looked out the window and straight into Cal Lightfoot's stoic face. After staring at each other for a moment, both men looked away. The van moved ahead into traffic, and Logan turned back to Skylar. "Never seen him before," he told the driver.

"Need I tell you that I'm very close to having a nervous breakdown?" Skylar murmured close to his ear.

"Only after I beat the flaming hell out of you for disobeying orders," she was told. "You were to change taxis once, go back to your restaurant, and wait for me to call you there."

"I did wait for your call."

"You were supposed to send a taxi for me, Skylar, not personally ride shotgun. You could have been killed." His hands descended upon her shoulders. He shook her furiously for a moment. "If the driver of that damned van hadn't broken in when he did, you would have been dead. There was very little I could have done to protect you." There was an underlying panic in the angry words tumbling from his lips. Skylar was stunned by his reaction.

"I'm—I'm sorry," she managed to get in the second he stopped for air. "I was afraid you would need help after seeing the doctor. You can be assured I debated the wisdom of coming for you or simply sending someone."

"It was a damned fool thing to do, regardless of how long you debated the issue. Terrorists have no feelings, honey. They live only to destroy. They have passed beyond conscience. *If* the van hadn't interfered, *if* the garbage truck and the other car, and eventually the police, hadn't interfered, we, along with the driver of this taxi, would probably be in about a billion different little pieces by now."

"Must you be so gruesome?"

"Yes. If it will make you stick to the plan of action we agreed on, then I'll be unbelievably gruesome."

He continued holding her, as much for support as for the comforting touch of her body against his. His side was aching like hell, and he knew for certain he was running a temperature.

"Talk to me, honey," he said in a low voice against Skylar's ear. "I have to be alert enough to change back to 'Aunt Katherine' once we get to your car."

"But the police stopped the baldheaded man."

"I know. But I happen to remember there being two of them the other night. I'm pretty sure I managed to shoot one of them, but how seriously is still anybody's guess."

"Oh, God!" All she wanted was to get to her apartment, get inside, and lock all three locks on her front door.

She looked up at him with bewildered eyes.

"How in God's name can you stand working like this? You walk a razor's edge every single day of your life. Don't you ever find yourself wanting to go to bed without programing yourself to wake up at the slightest noise? Don't you ever want to know what it would be like to marry and have children? Don't you ever want to settle down in one spot longer than a few days . . . or weeks?"

Tears were streaming unheeded down her cheeks as the present and the past became one huge collage of unhappiness. She'd loved Tim with all her heart. But she'd learned, to her surprise, that even love, without the proper nurture and care, can wither. It doesn't exactly die, but it becomes dormant. She had withdrawn, covering herself with a protective shell—to protect herself where Tim was concerned.

Tim. A happy, laughing Tim when he'd placed his ring on her finger. A defiant, angry Tim when she'd given him back the ring.

"Don't do this to me, Sky," he'd yelled at her. "I need you. I need your beauty, your goodness, to come to when I can't take it any longer."

"And just how long do you think I can supply the sunshine, the happiness, for us both, Tim? Where will I go for my refills? Who'll give me a boost when I'm exhausted from keeping you entertained and happy?"

He hadn't known what to say—and Skylar hadn't known what to do to change the direction of their lives. In the days that followed she finally realized that directional changes for two people had to be considered and shared by both.

Three weeks later, she stood silent, her heart ready to burst with grief as she stared down into the lifeless face of the man she'd loved.

In the gathering of stunned friends, relatives, and co-workers, she'd listened to words of praise at what a fine officer Tim had been. Fearless . . . the kind of partner everyone wanted when things were tight. Big deal, she'd wanted to scream at them all. Big deal. None of the virtues of being the perfect officer had saved his life. Quite the contrary—those same virtues had resulted in his death.

"Skylar? It's all right now. Everything's all right." Logan held her close, one large hand gently smoothing its way over her back and shoulders. She was hurting, bad. Her body was stiff with tension and pain. He could feel it in her and he felt it for her. But there was nothing in the world he could do to stop it.

His expression became one of mockery as he reflected on the godawful ironies of life.

Earlier in the evening he'd been like a child, almost giddy with the happiness at the mere thought of where his feelings for Skylar were headed. Even on the plane, he'd been taken with her. She pleased him . . . honest to God pleased him. He could listen for hours to her talk. She was funny, capable of turning the simplest incident into a humorous event. She was beautiful, she was charming—when she wasn't raking him over the coals, he mused—she was cute . . .

What the hell do you think you're doing? the mocking voice chimed in. So the woman pleases you. So what? Don't let yourself be caught up by a pair of dancing green eyes, and hair that glistens like liquid copper.

"I'm okay now," Skylar finally said. She felt like a first-class idiot. But people trying to kill her had a unique way of making her lose her cool. She cast a shy glance at Logan as she eased herself off his chest. "I haven't even asked how you're feeling or what the doctor told you."

"My, my," he teased. "Ms. Dennis forgetting her manners. Tsk, tsk." He kissed her on the tip of her nose and wiped away the remaining tear clinging to the corner of her eye. "Unbeknowst to us, there was a tiny fragment of steel in the wound. It caused an infection, and is responsible for making me feel

153

like holy hell for the greater part of today and this evening. I have antibiotics and something to help me sleep. I declined the sleeping pills, but the doctor insisted."

Skylar smiled. "Very good. Sounds like you haven't left out a single thing. How are you feeling at the moment?"

"Miserable. I'm fairly positive I'm running a temperature."

She reached out and laid the back of her hand against his brow. "You do feel warm. We'll get you in bed and started on the antibiotics as soon as we get home."

"Yes, ma'am," Logan murmured meekly.

"Ha!" Skylar hooted, thinking how remarkable the human mind and body were. They'd just came through a terrifying experience, yet here they were, acting as normal as if they were returning from a football game. It was amazing.

Once back in the VW, Logan lost a portion of his good humor as he grunted and cursed during his transition to "Aunt Katherine." "If I never do another thing in my entire lifetime, I promise to present you with a new car, Skylar Dennis. This tin can is the pits."

"Sticks and stones . . ." She grinned at him. "Besides, I like it. We've been together since my first year in college. I could never trade her off."

"Indeed not." Logan smiled flintily. "Who the hell would take 'her'?"

"I'll have you know, this is still a very—er—worthy vehicle."

"In a pig's eye! It only runs in fits and starts, which will probably wind up getting you killed, and if that doesn't happen, someone will probably run over you. It's an accident on four wheels, just waiting to happen."

Skylar smiled as she turned into the parking lot of the apartment complex. "I wouldn't be too hard on her, if I were . . . Logan!"

"What?" He grunted the response, his hands busy adjusting the gray wig with the chignon at the nape.

"Do you see what I see?"

"Obviously not," he snapped. "But I do feel a damned pin sticking into my scalp. Will you hurry up and get me the hell out of this garb?"

"Logan Gant, will you please stop carrying on like an idiot?" she threw at him. "Look over there, parked under that oak tree."

Logan did look. He saw a van, the same color and make as the one involved in the skirmish on Canal Boulevard. A man stepped from behind the vehicle.

"That looks exactly like the van and the driver," Skylar said amazed. "Can you beat that? Apparently that man lives right here in the same apartments. Don't you think we should say something to him? Like maybe . . . thanks, or something?"

"Oh," Logan said unconcerned, still fiddling with his wardrobe, "I suspect you'll get a chance to do a lot more than just thank him. Hurry up, honey, and let me get out of here. I feel lousy as hell."

"Sorry." She threw him a curious look, then opened the door and stepped out. The man from the van was walking directly toward them, and Skylar wasn't certain what she should do. Could he possibly be one of the terrorists? She ducked her head into the VW. "Logan, that man is coming over here. What do we do?"

"Talk to him, honey. Better yet, get him to help you unload that wheelchair."

"But, Logan," she protested. "What if he's . . . you know . . . involved?"

"Why, then, I'll simply trade places with him and let you push him off the balcony and into the pool. How's that?"

"Logan Gant, will you please be serious? What if he whips out a damned bomb and blows us all to hell and back?

"Skylar!" Logan exclaimed with suspect horror.

"Begging your pardon, Ms. Dennis," a cool, precise voice spoke from directly behind Skylar, "but I'm fresh out of bombs at the moment. However, I do know how to take some fuel and a bottle and a rag and make something that will do fairly well in an emergency. Will that qualify as a bomb?"

Skylar swung around to meet her "enemy," the top of her head hitting the upper edge of the car roof with a resounding thud. "Ohh!" She put both hands to her head, blinking through thousands of imaginary stars in an effort to see this perfect stranger who knew her name.

"Wh-Who are you?" she asked, glancing from an unperturbed Logan to the newcomer.

"My name is Cal Lightfoot. I was sent to sort of keep an eye on you, Ms. Dennis." He smiled faintly. "I must admit, you gave me a bad time back there."

A frown creased the smooth skin of Skylar's brow. Look after her? What on earth was he talking about? "Exactly who sent you to look after me?"

"The agency, ma'am," Cal explained. "I work for the same agency that Logan does."

"You work for the same agency that Logan does," she repeated slowly, not knowing whether to laugh or cry. She only knew one thing. She was angry. Not in just a little bit of a snit, but angry enough to singe the hinges off a metal box! "Thank you, Mr. Lightfoot," she said crisply. "I appreciate your concern." She turned and looked in at dear, sweet "Aunt Katherine." "As for you, you deceitful toad, I hope you croak dead on the spot. If not, you can rest assured I'll do everything within my power to kill you!" She spun on her heel and stalked toward the entrance of the apartments, pointedly ignoring the two gaping men.

CHAPTER NINE

Skylar entered the apartment like a small tornado. She was furious. Absolutely furious. Logan Gant had allowed her to make a complete fool of herself by letting her think they'd been in imminent danger from the baldheaded man in the dark sedan. That had been his first mistake.

The second one had been in not telling her that his agency had assigned someone to watch her. In her totally irrational mood at the moment, she wasn't ready to accept help from an organization she abhorred. "And that probably makes me the biggest fool of the year!" she muttered.

She paused in the middle of the living room, when it suddenly occurred to her just how close to dying she and Logan had come. Dear Lord!

Her knees began to shake. Then her arms . . . and lastly her hands. From her extremities it spread to the trunk of her body. With great difficulty she managed to stumble over to the sofa and collapse. She immediately pulled her knees toward her chest in the fetal position and closed her eyes.

A sudden knocking on the door failed to rouse Skylar. She heard it, but she simply couldn't find the strength to get up and answer. Seconds later she heard voices: Logan's, Cal Lightfoot's, and Francine's. She heard someone laugh.

What a crock! she thought derisively.

She was in a state of severe shock, and her friends were having a party. She was dying and they were celebrating. The door opened and the party entered.

"Skylar?" Francine called her friend's name the moment she saw her huddled on the sofa, then rushed forward. "Skylar? What's wrong?"

Suddenly the space behind Francine was filled with Logan's face—framed by the white lace collar under his chin, and the snow-white wig on his head—and that of Cal Lightfoot. Skylar closed her eyes again. She didn't want to see anyone. She wanted to savor the newness of her anger, wanted to squeeze the last drop of nectar from the bitter fruit of deception. She also wanted a chance to try and deal with the knowledge that if Cal hadn't intervened, at this moment she could be dead.

"Skylar?" Logan said roughly. He pushed past Francine and dropped to one knee beside the sofa. "Can you speak? Are you all right? Talk to me, dammit!"

"Logan." Cal laid a reassuring hand on his friend's shoulder. "I think she's in shock." He looked at a startled Francine. "Is there some brandy in the kitchen?"

"Yes, I think so." She got to her feet and hurried away. In seconds she was back, and handed the drink to Logan. "Try this."

He slipped an arm beneath Skylar's head, then placed the glass to her lips. "Take a sip of this for me, honey," he instructed her.

With all her might Skylar wanted to tell him to take his brandy and highball it straight to hell! But at that precise moment she was trembling so badly her teeth sounded like castanets. She would have taken a drink from the devil if it would have calmed her shivering body.

Cal Lightfoot caught Francine's eye and nodded his head toward the kitchen. Once there, he introduced himself, surprising her by knowing her name.

"But how?" she asked surprised. "We've never met."

"Do you know anything about what's going on with Logan?" he questioned her sharply.

"You mean about how he 'persuaded' Sky-

161

lar to help him on the flight from Dallas? That
he's a spy and that there are terrorists looking
for him—probably to kill him?"

Cal grinned. "I suppose that about covers it.
I'll make a deal with you."

"What kind of a deal?"

"If you'll put on a pot of coffee, then I'll fill
you in on a few of the details—at least, what
details I'm allowed to give you. Deal?"

"Deal."

In the living room Skylar was lying back on
the sofa pillows Logan had jammed behind
her head. She was staring at him as if she'd
never seen him before.

Logan felt like the absolute lowest form of
life on God's green earth. This slip of a woman
had risked her own life in order to help him—
more than once—and now she was regarding
him with such utter contempt that he felt like
disappearing into a hole. She'd gotten down
all the brandy and the trembling had left her
body. Now Logan was faced with the problem
of how to remove the utter contempt for him
he saw in her eyes, and get her to talk to him.

Suddenly an idea occurred to him. Not a
very honorable one, but he didn't have time
to quibble.

"Skylar, I'd like to sit here and tease you out
of your anger, honey, but I can't. The doctor
advised me to go straight to bed when I got

home. Of course I thought that was a ridiculous idea at the time, but now I can see that he's correct."

He made as if to get up, grabbed at his injured side, then caught himself by throwing out his hand and grabbing hold of the back of the sofa.

"Logan?" Skylar sat up, her hands reaching out to him and grasping his arm in a futile effort to support him. "Are you all right?"

"I'm not so sure, honey."

"We'd better get you to bed." She scrambled to her feet, keeping a steady arm around his waist. "Can you walk or do you want me to call your friend in to help you?"

Logan looked deep into her eyes. "I'd rather you help me, Skylar. Will you?"

She paused in her fussing. "Are you really in such terrible shape, Logan, or are you up to another of your little tricks?"

"Does it really matter, honey?" He straightened to his full height, pulling Skylar up with him, maneuvering her in front of him so she wasn't pressing against his bad side.

"If you're deceiving me just to laugh at me, then it does matter."

"Whatever I've done, Skylar, where you're concerned, has been done to protect you . . . always. You must believe me."

"We're talking about your friend Mr. Light-foot, aren't we?"

Logan nodded. "In that first conversation I had with Allen Deen, the Chief of Orka, I asked him to put a man on you. Can't you understand that I had to do that? I felt guilty enough about bursting into your life the way I did. If something were to happen to you because of my actions, I think I'd kill myself. At any rate, I was fairly certain no one had traced me here to your place, but I couldn't be sure. I wanted the assurance that you were protected day and night. Allen suggested Cal, and I agreed. He's one of the best."

"Next to you, you mean," Skylar said quietly. "You're the best, Logan Gant, by anybody's standards."

A huge knot lodged in Logan's throat. Perhaps she wasn't aware of it, he thought, but the feelings revealed in her eyes were enough to cause any man to ditch his climbing gear, and go running up Mt. Everest! She was looking at him as if she could eat him up, and he was about the most willing creature on earth.

He caught her face between his hands. "Skylar Dennis, you're turning me inside out. Me, a man with a reputation for loving and leaving the women, a man who lets nothing interfere with his job—who's seen enough horror created by mankind to last twenty men. A man who—and only one or two people know this—once knew a woman's love and swore never to let his heart become involved again. But in all my days upon this earth, I've never known a person to give so unselfishly of herself as you do. You've become a very large problem in my life. And solving that problem is going to be the most difficult decision I've ever made."

"Problems usually have a way of working themselves out, Logan," Skylar said softly. She stood on her tiptoes and touched her lips to his. "Now, let's get you to bed before you drop."

With a helping hand from Cal, Logan was put to bed and given a dose of antibiotics and a sleeping pill, fussing and complaining every step of the way.

"I swear." Skylar glowered at him. "—if you don't learn to control your damnable temper, I'm going to have your mouth wired shut."

A scorching look brought nothing but smirks from Cal, Francine, and Skylar. "Don't look so pleased with this little party, Lightfoot. You might find yourself in a similar situation one day, and I can assure you, I'll be at ringside applauding—for the other side."

"We Indians are famous for holding out, Gant," Cal retorted solemnly. "You, on the other hand, look to me to be folding."

* * *

The next morning while Skylar was preparing breakfast for her two guests—she'd insisted Cal sleep on the sofa—the phone rang.

"Ms. Dennis?" a strange voice asked.

Skylar was gripping the receiver so firmly her knuckles turned white. Cold, stark fear raced in waves from the top of her head to the tip of her toes. Had they found Logan after all?

"Who is this, please?" she said briskly.

"I'm interested in acquiring a Hawk. I was told you might know where I could purchase one."

She was silent. Was this really the man Logan had spoken with or was it a hoax? She recalled the code words that Logan had taught her. "Is there a Rainbow in the sky today?"

"A lovely one. I was just admiring it."

"Are you a student of the native Americans?"

"Indeed I am. I find the Apache tribe to be especially interesting."

"The Apache? What a coincidence, so do I. Perhaps we can do business together after all."

"I need to speak with Hawk. Is he there?"

"He's resting. There's been some complications with his injury."

There was a sharp intake of breath on the other end of the line. "Is it serious?" the voice asked.

"Nothing some rest and antibiotics won't take care of. He saw a doctor late last night. A small bullet fragment had set up an infection. Fortunately we caught it before it had gotten too far out of hand. Er . . . Cochise is here. Would you like to speak with him?"

"Please."

Skylar called Cal to the phone, then went to check on Logan. He didn't stir when she eased the door open and went into the room. She walked on over to the bed and stood staring down at him.

Apparently the fever had made him restless. The pastel sheets were nothing more than tangled ropes, twisted about his body like pale blue vines. Navy briefs served as pajamas, and Skylar knew instinctively he'd kept them on simply out of courtesy to her. Logan didn't strike her as a man who went in for sleeping attire.

Her eyes moved slowly over the length of him, looking their fill at long, lean legs, the calves and thighs muscled and firm. His legs as well as the rest of him were a delicious tan, bringing a rush of envy from Skylar. He stayed year round the color she tried to capture a few months each year. Being a red-head, however, her quest was usually in vain.

She looked at the wide bandage; the injury would leave a scar. The white of the bandage was intensified, nestled as it was along one side amid the dark pelt of hair on his chest. Dark, thick hair . . . inviting the teasing touch of her fingertips . . . why, if she were to touch . . .

"What's going on in that beautiful head of yours, Ms. Dennis?"

Skylar gave a start and jerked back her out-stretched hand, a hot flush of color stealing over her cheeks as she found Logan's openly appraising gaze on her. "Y-you must have spent a restless night. Your bed's a mess."

"What would you say if I were to tell you that I spent the night dreaming I was making love to you?"

Skylar felt as if she had stopped breathing as their gazes locked and held. The warmth pouring from the blue depths was as potent as if his hands were caressing her body, touch-ing, molding, then smoothing their way over her till every inch of her was known to him. She sucked in her breath, her nipples turning to pebbled hardness . . . the fantasy so real she was becoming heady with the sensation.

Logan raised himself onto one elbow, then reached out and caught hold of her hand, drawing her down beside him. He knew and understood the look in her eyes with stunning accuracy, just as she knew what was going on in his mind.

With infinite gentleness he dropped back against his pillow and cradled her head on his shoulder, his fingers threading in and out of the auburn curls. "You do know I'm going to make love to you before this is all over, don't you?"

"Yes. And as weird as it may sound, I want you so much it makes me dizzy. Yet I'm terrified that when it's done, my heart will be broken."

"I know." Logan nodded wisely. "It's my work, isn't it?"

"Yes. If I live to be a hundred years old, Logan, I can never accept it. You saw what happened to me last night. Can you imagine what I'd be like if I had to think of you being constantly involved in that sort of thing? Nor can I allow us to establish some sort of hit-and-miss relationship that will tie me up in knots for years and keep me from enjoying any sort of normal life. Does that make any sense?"

"More sense than I care to admit." He sighed. "Believe me, honey, I wasn't looking to find anyone like you. In fact"—he half grinned—"I considered myself something of an oddity. I was immune. Ha!"

169

"Well, Mr. Immune," Skylar began, letting part of her fantasy come to life by burying her fingers in the dark hair on his chest, "the reason I came in here in the first place is to tell you that a very nervous man called Rainbow is, at this moment, talking with Cal."

"Rainbow?" he said alertly.

"The same. I assume he's the head cheese of your organization?"

"Yes. Does he want to talk with me?"

"I told him you were sleeping, that you were taking antibiotics and being given sleeping pills. Do you want to talk with him?"

"Cal can handle it. If it's for me personally, Cal will call me."

"May I ask exactly what the name of your agency is?"

"Is it important that you know?"

"It's not a matter of life and death." She frowned. "On the other hand, I think by now you should be able to trust me."

"Trusting you is a foregone conclusion, honey. I knew I could trust you when I spent nearly two hours the other night backtracking and winding my way to you. Stop and think, Skylar. Do you honestly think I would have come to you for help if I hadn't known for certain I could trust you?"

She shrugged. "I suppose not. But what has

that got to do with whether or not you tell me name of the agency?"

"There's an old saying, something about what you don't know won't hurt you. In this particular instance truer words were never spoken. If you don't know anything about me or my work, then there's no way you can make a mistake and let something slip that will later come back to haunt you."

"Since my circle of friends do not include international terrorists or international spies —with the exception of you and Cal—it makes no sense at all to leave me stumbling around dumb as a post. Tell me the name of the agency, Logan?" she repeated in a steely voice.

He began to laugh, and the movement of his chest caused Skylar's head to bob up and down like an apple in a tub of water at Halloween. She switched positions enough to stare crossly at him. "May one ask what's so funny?"

"Indeed 'one' may. My agency is called Orka."

"Orka?" she repeated. "Who on earth chose that title?"

"Oh, dear." Logan grinned. "You don't like it?" God! She was like a steady ray of sunshine beaming down on him. He wouldn't even let himself consider the day when he wouldn't be with her.

"Oh . . . I suppose it's okay. I was hoping for the CIA or FAT or Man from UNCLE. Even plain old FBI would be better than 'Orka.' It reminds me of that slimy vegetable."

"I'll pass on your assessment of title to Rainbow," Logan teased her. "Being the stickler for details that he is, he might well change the name to ZAP or something else equally electrifying."

Skylar propped herself up on her elbows. "You look and sound one hundred percent better this morning."

"I hate to admit it, but I'm feeling great."

"Why do you hate to admit it, silly?"

"Because I'm afraid you'll desert me if I recover too quickly. I haven't forgotten that last night the only way I could get you speaking to me was to pretend to be near death."

"That was a mean and underhanded thing to do, Logan Gant, but under the circumstances I forgive you." She pushed herself into a sitting position. "Now, do you feel like eating at the table or would you like a tray in here?"

"I'll get up. And if you don't mind, please ask Cal to step in here."

"Business, mmmmm?"

172

" 'Fraid so, honey."

"How long have you been with the agency, Logan?"

"Fourteen years."

"And we've known each other for almost three days. Amazing. Have you always been involved in—er—"

"Covert activities?"

"Yes."

"For the last fourteen years, yes. There were three years before that when I worked primarily in the control office learning the ropes." He looked directly at Skylar. "I haven't regretted a single day I've been with the agency."

A heavy feeling of despair wrapped its cloying fingers around Skylar's heart as she listened to his words.

He didn't regret a single day. . . . *She* regretted every single day of his association with the agency.

Even a fool could see it was a moot point.

Around nine o'clock she called the restaurant and told Hubie she wasn't feeling well.

"Does it have anything to do with the mysterious houseguest you've acquired?" he teased.

"Of course," she continued the theme. "I've taken a live-in lover, and we're hoping

173

to make the *Guinness Book of World Records* as the couple making love for the longest continuous period of time."

"Oh. I thought it was something interesting."

"Having trouble with Caroline?"

"Don't I always?"

"So you do. Well, not to worry, I'll be in this evening. Okay?"

"Get here when you can, honey. I know it's important or you wouldn't be missing work."

As the day wore on, Skylar found herself besieged with every conceivable notion regarding Logan Gant. She argued that her interest in him was purely platonic. He was kind and gentle, in spite of his distasteful profession.

Your mind may think platonic, sweetie, her conscience hooted, but your body has designs resembling flashing red lights turned directly on his gorgeous hunk of masculinity.

Okay, so it's infatuation . . . with highly sexual overtones. Is that any better?

No.

Every time she tried to rationalize the strange rapport she'd developed with a man she'd known only a few days, she came up with huge blanks in her analysis.

Even Cal was acting as if she and Logan were more than just friends.

"Your idea to dress him as your aunt was really fantastic," he told Skylar as the four of them—Cal, Skylar, Logan, and Francine— played cards. "I almost cracked up when I saw you two struggling to get this character in that VW."

"Glad you enjoyed yourself, Cal," Logan remarked. "I'll bet twenty-five dollars." He selected the proper amount of chips and tossed them into the center of the table.

Francine studied her cards. "I'll raise you ten. And just for the record"—she smiled sweetly at Logan—"I was all for pushing your tush into the pool. You have a terrible temper. Are you staying or folding, Sky?"

Skylar frowned, her teeth chewing away at her bottom lip. "I'm thinking, Fran, I'm thinking." Finally she pushed forward some chips. "I'm staying, and I'll raise you fifty."

"Now, Sky, honey," Cal began. "Why don't you and me pool our resources and become partners? That way we could really give those two a licking."

Skylar eyed his pitifully lacking stack of poker chips. "I'm afraid I can't afford you."

Logan laughed, and Cal bemoaned the plight of the world that allowed women to be on equal footing with men, a chauvinistic remark that immediately had both women hot and heavy after his hide.

The battle was going fast and furious, and Logan was sitting back egging on the girls when the doorbell rang. Immediately, absolute silence overtook the foursome. Skylar rose to her feet, glancing uncertainly toward each man.

They both moved like lightning, taking positions that afforded them views of the door. At a nod from Logan, Skylar placed her hand on the knob. "Yes?"

"Ms. Dennis? Watch the bottom of your door, please."

Skylar looked down just as a business card slid through the narrow space. She bent and was about to pick it up, when her wrist was caught in a grip that was paralyzing.

"Don't touch that!" Logan hissed. "Get back. Duck behind the sofa." She did as he told her, then watched mystified while he and Cal went to their knees and studied the card.

"What on earth are they looking for?" Francine whispered. She was hovering beside Skylar, equally puzzled. "Do they expect it to take wings and fly? Maybe they think it's a bomb." As soon as the words were out of her mouth, it dawned on each of them that that was exactly what Logan and Cal were looking for.

"Dear Lord!" Skylar shuddered, knowing she would never forget the sight of the two men as they struggled to come to a decision, a decision that could take all their lives or one that could let them continue to live. She caught Francine's hand and squeezed it. "This has to be a nightmare. A horrible, horrible nightmare. Things like this really don't happen to people." But deep in her heart she knew they did. And worse yet, for all the reasons she'd dredged up for disliking the activities Logan was involved in, including Tim's death as well, the "profound" importance of such work finally became more than men merely getting their kicks out of a way of life she considered rather juvenile. In the present world it was an avenue of work that was a must if mankind was to survive.

When Logan reached for the card, Skylar held her breath. She saw him turn and smile, saw him clap Cal on the shoulder—saw them rise to their feet. Only then did she let out the air that was threatening to explode inside her chest.

The door was opened, and a short, broad-shouldered man with sandy hair stood with a hand braced on either side of the doorjamb. "It sure took you fellas long enough to look over a simple business card." A huge grin broke out over his pleasant face as he shook hands with both men.

Logan closed the door, then turned to Skylar and Francine. "Ladies, I'd like you to meet our newest pigeon—Allen Deen, fantastic at checkers, but lousy at poker. Allen, meet Ms. Skylar Dennis and Ms. Francine Winter."

CHAPTER TEN

With Logan, Cal, and Allen in New Orleans, Skylar began to wonder if anybody was left in Virginia to mind the shop.

"Is it common for several of your . . . people to be in one location?" she asked Allen. It was the evening of the second day of his visit, and he was cooling his heels in Skylar's kitchen, waiting till time to take Francine out to dinner.

"It depends on the circumstances," Allen told her, filching another piece of ham from the huge chef's salad she was preparing. "Mmmm, this is delicious."

Skylar regarded him resignedly. "Since you've eaten almost a pound, I kind of got the idea you liked it. I'm surprised you don't just call Francine and cancel your dinner date."

"No way," he said determinedly. "I happen to think your neighbor is a very neat lady. But tell me something. Is there someone special in her life?"

"A man, you mean."

"Yes."

Skylar grinned. "I wish I could tell you there was, but I can't. Why?"

"You're nosy."

"True. But how am I ever to know anything if I don't ask questions?"

This time he grinned, albeit rather sheepishly. "Do you believe in love at first sight, Skylar?"

"Oops!" She paused cutting cheese in long strips. "Are you saying what I think you're saying?"

" 'Fraid so. It'd make it all a whole lot easier, though, if I thought I had a chance."

"Has it occurred to you to ask *her* if there's a chance for you?" Skylar slowly and carefully asked him, as if talking to a child. Men! Honestly!

"What if she says no?" He had a look of such pathetic hopelessness on his face, Skylar reached out and patted him on the shoulder. "Don't worry. You'll find a way."

"I doubt it. I was hoping you'd help me."

Skylar looked up at the ceiling and slowly shook her head. "You've got to be kidding. You've been involved for years in a career that requires nerves of steel. Yet here you are, standing in my kitchen, telling me you're afraid to tell a woman you care for her."

"Will you sound her out for me?" Allen persisted.

"You do know that men in your particular line of work don't rate very high on my scale, don't you?"

"It's not your scale I'm interested in, honey."

"Touché." Skylar laughed. "I'll see what I can do for you."

"Thanks. Now I think I'll go have a few words with Logan."

"Are you sending him away?"

Allen turned and looked pityingly at her. "Not today . . . and probably not tomorrow, Skylar. But the day is coming when he's going to go. Isn't there some way you can come to grips with that?"

"I really don't see how," she whispered.

Allen ran Logan to ground in Cal's van. Cal was out jogging. "It's time we talked."

"Shoot."

"Orka agents have recently been singled out for random hits in an attempt to cripple our manpower."

"It doesn't take a genius to figure that out, Allen. Is that all you found out when you called in?"

"Not at all. But what I'm about to tell you is so fantastic you might not believe it at first."

181

Logan regarded his friend for a moment. "Let's hear it."

"As you know, the Middle East is a continuous hotbed of turmoil. In days past, if nothing better came along, they'd argue about the weather. At any rate, word has it—and very reliable word at that—there's going to be a new round of peace talks."

"Peace talks in that part of the world are daily fare."

"True. However, something's a little different with this situation. As you know, there's a conference of five free-world nations about to begin in Japan. Another conference, supposedly to sell the idea of robotically manned space stations, with some hefty peace negotiations thrown in for good measure, is geared up to begin in the next week or two. Last, but not least, we have a third group that will be representing three nations." He named the U.S. and two other Middle Eastern nations. One was an ally of the States, the other a country sectioned and divided by warring factions. "This last one will be taking place on a resort island off the east coast of Florida. From the information we have gathered all these conferences or meetings will open within three days of each other."

"You're losing me, Allen." Logan frowned.

"If it's peace they're seeking, then why make war on our agents?"

"The character chasing you isn't now, nor has he ever been, interested in peace."

"Then the connection?"

"Assassination. An attempt to sabotage the talks."

"They changed the faces but the rhetoric stays the same. But just for the record, who is to be assassinated? And which country is the culprit?"

"If we knew that, my friend, then there'd be no need for us to be sitting in this van, trying to make two and two come out as five. It's supposed to look as if Israel is up to dirty tricks, but we think another faction is responsible. All we've been able to come up with is rumor to the effect that a little-known but especially brutal faction is going to hit one of the conferences."

"And of course they wouldn't think of letting anyone in on their little secret, would they?" Logan muttered savagely.

"Why, I do believe you've had previous encounters with friends and relations of the culprits."

"You could say that. However, all these little groups have one thing in common. They have no more regard for human life than they do for a fly. They'd blow up their mother if it would further their cause." Logan sat staring into space, his mind grappling with the different angles to the problem just presented to him by Allen. "First thing I need to do is fly to Virginia. I need to take several hours and do some serious studying of head shots and personality profiles. Somewhere there has to be something on the clown who tried to kill me."

"What about Cal? Want him to hang around for a couple more days?"

"I'd feel better if he did."

"Then that's the way we'll leave it. By the way, he's having dinner with Francine and me this evening. He's also taking the night off, so you and Skylar can have some time to yourselves."

"Thanks, Allen. At the moment I need time with Skylar more than anything."

Allen caught the back of his neck with one hand in an uncertain gesture. "I don't envy you that confrontation. She's adamantly against the agency, isn't she?"

Logan nodded. "She used to be engaged to an undercover cop. Apparently he was really gung-ho . . . you know the type. At any rate, they broke up and he was killed a short time later. Since then she's developed a dedicated hatred for law enforcement of all shapes and sizes."

Allen looked pityingly at his friend. He saw

something in Logan Gant's eyes he'd never seen there before. He'd been fortunate enough to find someone to love. Would his career destroy that love and deny him that one last chance for happiness?

Skylar was seated in the old-fashioned rocker in her bedroom, her hands folded in her lap and her ankles crossed. She'd been in the same position for the past fifteen minutes. One thing she had to say about Logan: When it came to cooking and keeping an eye on the clock, he was a complete dud.

She'd been given strict orders not to come near the kitchen, or else she would have gone and tried to help him.

"Why don't we go to Hubie's for dinner?" she asked him when he suggested they make dinner that evening something special. "We serve fantastic food, and frankly, I'd like to show you the place. I'm rather proud of it."

"I'm sure it's a very nice restaurant, and someday I hope to eat there. In the meantime I want to wait another day. If no one's made an effort to find me by then, I think it's safe to assume they've given up."

"How can you stand to let the likes of that evil man control your life?" she asked curiously. "Doesn't it bother you when you're forced to hide like a criminal?"

"Frankly, honey, it's been years since I've had to take cover. Getting wounded isn't an everyday occurrence, you know. There's something else that's different about this time."

"What's that?"

"You. I've never had such a sexy little red-head to hide out with me. Makes all the difference in the world."

"You refuse to be serious about this, don't you? In fact, there's no point in trying to discuss it at all, is there?"

Logan teased her chin with his knuckles. "No, my little stubborn one, there really isn't. I have certain priorities in life, just as you do. Now, what would you like for dinner?"

That had ended the discussion, and Skylar had been left with nothing but disappointment—though the more she thought about it, the more she wondered just what it was she wanted Logan to tell her. At this point in their relationship, they were . . . friends. Rather close, but friends nevertheless. As such, she had no legitimate right to make demands on him. In fact, she continued the pep talk, she was probably reading a whole lot more into the entire situation than there really was.

The door swung open. Logan stood before her dressed in the dark gray sport jacket and light-colored pants. The shirt was white, and

Skylar smiled. She had a suspicion ties probably went the same route as did pajamas in Logan's life.

He walked over to her, took her hand in his, then raised it to his lips. "You are a vision of loveliness, Ms. Dennis. An absolute vision."

"Why, thank you, Mr. Gant."

"Would you join me for a glass of wine before dinner?"

"I'd love to." She smiled. "May I also compliment you on your attire? Quite an improvement over your pink-and-green checked creation—not to mention your 'Aunt Katherine' ensemble."

He took her by the arm and escorted her from the room. "It all has to do with my nose." He smiled benignly down at her.

"Your nose?"

"Of course. It lends an air of distinction— sort of sets me apart from the masses. Why, even in rags I'd be noticeable."

"You certainly would," Skylar agreed, unable to control the laughter gurgling in her throat.

Logan picked up a glass of wine from a silver tray on the coffee table. "Do I detect ridicule, Ms. Dennis?"

"Certainly not, Mr. Gant, certainly not." She sipped the wine, wrinkling her nose appreciatively. "Nice. Obviously something you bought. My taste in wines is atrocious."

Logan said something clever and Skylar laughed. She lost track of time, and wanted to keep it that way. In her heart she had the most awful feeling of dread—and it involved Logan.

The succulent steak, baked potato, and salad he served for dinner could have been so much hay for all the attention Skylar paid to it. She ate and smiled and talked, but beneath it all she simply wanted whatever it was he was holding back from her to be gotten out in the open. The kind of games he indulged in were too much for her.

Together they cleared the table and put the dishes in the dishwasher. Everything went off like clockwork. Even down to the cassette he popped into the tape deck and the slow, throbbing music that gently filled the background. When he opened his arms to her, she went unhesitatingly into them. She was enfolded into and against the entire width and breadth of his being, and she was positive that at any second her heart was going to break. Friends? A tiny voice reminded her of her earlier reflections . . . no way.

Their bodies became one in sway and time to the music. Logan was a good dancer and Skylar hadn't the slight bit of trouble following his lead. "Next time we dance it'll be in a club. There'll be an orchestra and soft lights, and I want you to wear that green dress you wore the other night. Okay?"

"Are you certain there's going to be a next time?" she asked so softly he had to incline his head even more to hear her.

The arm encircling her tightened like a steel rope and the hands holding hers threatened to crush her fingers. His expression as he stared down at her would have been frightening if she hadn't known him. As it was, she knew that she wasn't the only one with a heavy heart. "There will be another evening, Skylar. And another and another and another. No matter what, don't ever stop believing that."

They continued dancing till Logan stopped, tipping her face so that he could look into her eyes. "I want to make love to you."

Skylar couldn't find the words to answer him. Heaven knew she wanted him, but she was so afraid of the aftermath. Afraid of the long, lonely days and nights when she'd cry out for him but he wouldn't be there. Of the dreams that would haunt her, wrenching sleep from her breast and leaving her with the dead, silent world of emptiness.

She turned, her hand still in his, and began walking toward the bedroom. If she waited ten thousand years, she would never find the words to express her feelings. Her only hope lay in showing him . . . in letting her body convey the wealth of her emotions to him.

When they reached the bedroom, Logan closed the door behind them and locked it. They walked on over to the bed and stopped. "Do you trust me?" He posed the question softly, and Skylar nodded, the glow from the one lamp leaving his face shadowy and unreadable.

"Yes."

"Good. Because if we have trust, then we have one of the most important things."

"What's the other thing, Logan?"

"Love. And God knows I do love you, Skylar Dennis."

She nodded happily. "I know. Just as I love you."

"I used to laugh when I'd hear people say they married their husbands after knowing them for only a few days or weeks. Now it doesn't seem funny at all. Would you marry me if I asked you?"

"Are you asking me?"

"You know, I honestly think I am. Will you?"

"One step at a time, Logan. Tonight's for the loving."

Without another word passing between

them, they undressed, their clothes dropping unheeded to the floor. When they were naked, Logan reached out and spanned her waist, smiling at her petiteness.

"There's nothing at all in excess about you, is there?"

Skylar smiled at the left-handed compliment, happy that she pleased him.

"I don't know. I've never thought about it."

He went to his knees, his large hands clasping the rounded flesh of her buttocks. Skylar gave a loud gasp when his lips touched her upper thighs. Her skin was like satin, Logan mused. Satiny . . . like magnolia blossoms. It was an expression he'd heard all his life. Now he knew what it meant. He felt her hands on his head, felt the tips of her fingers tugging at his hair, urging him closer to her. Without hesitating his tongue sought out that center of her being, and knew a moment of triumph when her body trembled.

He moved to her stomach, his lips and hands touching and smoothing the concave surface. Upward he worked his way, setting off ripple after ripple of minute explosions like millions of fireflies in a summer night's darkness.

The palm of his hand cupped a small, round breast, his thumb working the nipple back and forth with rapid strokes. Skylar sucked in her breath and held it till her brain was screaming for release. Her skin had become totally consumed with the need to feel his touch. She ran the moist tip of her tongue over lips gone dry with passion. Each nerve in her body was awakened to tingling awareness, each nerve ending quivering, pulsating its own delightful message of complete arousal.

When her legs gave way to the buffeting of passion and desire rushing over her, they fell to the bed. Breast to waist, hip to thigh, they lay still for a moment, savoring the newness of the unbelievable power of feeling they had created between them.

Of their own volition Skylar's hands became bold in her quest to please Logan as much as he was pleasing her. Her thoughts had become frenzied with the desire for only one act: that of creating for Logan the same unbelievable high of pleasure that was gripping her. She reveled in the sensation of her palms creating a gentle friction against the broad shoulders and wide back. The pleasurable sounds she was hearing from Logan brought her own enjoyment to an incredible peak. Giving and receiving, two halves creating one whole. Her hands dipped lower, skimming over the surface of his flat stomach, her fingertips darting and teasing their way to the velvety smoothness of his manhood.

Logan shuddered, his large frame quivering like a leaf in the wind. The fanciful notion came to him that holding Skylar in his arms and touching and loving her was comparable to holding a hot, licking flame, burning out of control.

"I love you, Skylar Dennis," he murmured, barely conscious of speaking, much less the actual words he'd spoken.

He touched his lips to her swollen nipples, his tongue flicking the tiny tips reverently. On up his questing mouth went, kissing and tasting the freshness of her skin, drinking her very own body scent—a scent that was burned into his memory. He kissed her then, his tongue invading her mouth and claiming its gentle passage just as he was about to claim her entire being as his own.

Skylar clasped him to her, her body opening to receive him. He entered her quickly; each was hungering for a fulfillment that only immediate release could bring. The foreplay having whetted their appetites so voraciously, only the tiniest spark of passion was needed to bring an explosion of gratification.

Sometime later, when the world had righted itself again, and the fires of passion had been banked, Logan told Skylar that he was leaving the next morning.

She was lying with her head on his chest, her outstretched hand resting on his arm. "I was wondering when you would tell me."

"You knew?"

"I knew something. I had a horrible feeling something was about to happen." She raised herself up on one elbow. "What will you be doing?"

Logan smiled tenderly at her. God! He loved her so very much, and he didn't want their relationship to be like the one she'd had with Tim. Logan only knew that when she hurt, he hurt; when she was unhappy, he was unhappy. "Nothing dangerous, I assure you. I'm going to spend some time going over personal profiles of known terrorists and enemies of the government."

"You really have files on people like that? I thought that was only in the movies."

"Quite the contrary. I'm sure all agencies dealing in covert activities, and many that don't, have files on all sorts of people. Some even that would surprise you."

"May I ask exactly what it is you're looking for?"

"Anything I can find on the baldheaded man. I don't recognize him, Cal didn't recognize him. That's unusual. Just about anyone

194

who's participated in any sort of subversive movement or activity anywhere in the world has a record and picture on file either at one of our agencies, or in other countries. Naturally we share a reciprocal arrangement wherein information is shared with other organizations abroad. However, from composite drawings and verbal descriptions, nothing has been forthcoming. We're still facing a blank."

"And you hope to dig and dig till you come up with something?"

"Correct." He teased the tip of her nose with one long finger. "You are very curious about why I'm going away. If I wanted to flatter myself, I'd think you're jealous."

"Then by all means flatter yourself, Logan."

"And what will you be doing while I'm away?" he asked silkily. "Will you be going to dinner or the theater with one of your boyfriends?"

"I did promise John I'd go to the Saints game on Sunday. That was when I was still angry at you for destroying my decorating scheme in the living room."

Logan tucked two strong fingers beneath her chin and tipped her head at an angle that enabled him to look directly into her eyes. "Why don't you tell John that you think it would be very risky for him to be seen with you?"

"Oh, my." She adopted a frightened pose. "Will you shoot him through the kneecaps . . . maybe torture him?"

He chuckled. "At least. Seriously, though, honey. I have no right to ask you not to see anyone."

"Logan, I—"

"Hear me out, Skylar. If this relationship is to even get off the ground, there's got to be trust on both sides. I know that right now you aren't very pleased with what I do. You've been hurt before because of a similar career. But all men aren't alike, honey."

"What are you trying to say?" She pushed away from him and sat in the middle of the bed, pulling the sheet up to her chest.

"I think you know, and you already resent it."

"That's not fair."

"I'm not condemning you, honey," Logan said patiently. "All I want you to do is try to accept that I simply have a job—a job like any other man. It's risky, but I know I'm good at it, and I don't take unnecessary risks. I'm not a glory seeker, Skylar. Keeping a low profile is very important in my profession."

Skylar picked at the sheet, trying to hide her disappointment, yet loving him even more for trying to reason with her. He continually amazed her with his sensitivity, with his gentleness. The incongruity between his profession and his personality was amazing. She finally raised her head and sought his gaze. "You must know I love you."

He looked down at the faint marks she'd left on his chest and at the perfect imprint of her teeth on his shoulder. "Very intense when *making love,* yes." He grinned. "As for *loving me* . . ." He looked steadily at her, his expression serious. "Yes, honey, I do know."

"That being the case, I really don't have much of a choice as to whether or not I try to understand, do I?"

Logan caught her hand and raised it to his lips. "Don't be bitter. . . . I'll make it all up to you, I promise." When she didn't respond, he pulled her to him, his lips claiming hers in a kiss that momentarily wiped away all doubts and fears. It was merely a placebo, and Logan knew it. But deep in his heart he knew he would use anything in his power to keep Skylar Dennis. He loved her with an intensity that was frightening. And even in the face of the odds Logan stood firm. He was the eternal optimist. He *would* have her.

CHAPTER ELEVEN

Without Logan's presence Skylar's warm, comfortable apartment became nothing more than a place to eat and sleep. It held memories that kept her heart prisoner and constantly reminded her that people should never make rash statements . . . such as who they would or would not love.

She remembered him in the kitchen, enjoying the chance to cook, then looking totally dismayed when he discovered how many pots and pans he'd dirtied in the creation of his "masterpieces," as he'd called them.

In the bathroom they'd taken a shower together well before daylight after that first night of lovemaking. Never again would she enter that small, ceramic-tiled space without seeing teasing blue eyes and brilliant white teeth smiling at her from a laughing tanned face.

The guest room, the bedroom, the living room. Skylar covered her face with her hands in an attempt to blot out Logan's ghost in every nook and cranny. Smiling, teasing . . . reminding her of the taste of his lips and the feel of his lovemaking.

It had been four days since he'd left, four days during which she'd gone around taking care of necessary chores . . . existing, more than living. How was it possible, she asked herself over and over, for her to have fallen in love with a man such as Logan? Hadn't she learned her lesson with Tim? Was there some hidden masochistic streak in her, controlling her thoughts and mind?

The second day after Logan's departure Skylar finally found time to take Tim's medal to Mrs. Dawson.

"I apologize for not getting here when I promised," she told the older woman, "but I had so much to catch up with on my return from Houston."

Mrs. Dawson patted her hand. "Not to worry, dear. What with my sister suddenly becoming ill, I was afraid you'd come by and I'd missed you." She waved Skylar to a chair, then took her seat on the small two-seater sofa and reached for the coffeepot resting on the tray on the coffee table. "I know you're probably in a great hurry—all you young people are these days—but a quick cup of coffee won't hurt you." She added the two spoons of sugar and the generous portion of milk that her guest was in the habit of taking, then handed the coffee to Skylar.

"You have a very good memory, Mrs. D."

"Because I remembered how you like your coffee?" She smiled, albeit a little sadly. "Why shouldn't I? Not too many months ago, you were to be my daughter-in-law. It's my duty to remember things like that. I want to be a good mother-in-law, you know."

"That's very thoughtful of you, Mrs. D." Skylar smiled. Privately she couldn't help but wonder if the poor woman was emotionally stable. Every time they spoke, either in person or on the phone, Skylar found the poor woman's mood swings varying from one extreme to the other.

By the time Skylar left, Mrs. Dawson was speaking of Tim as if he weren't dead, but simply at work. It was sad.

Allen, Logan, and several other members of the staff sat watching the large screen in the projection room of Orka headquarters. Face after face, along with accompanying personal profiles, came and went. When the final clip was finished, an atmosphere of discontent permeated the room. Little if any information had been gleaned from the process.

Logan raised his arms over his head and stretched, disappointment eating away at him. Under the circumstances he couldn't help feeling that he had more at stake than any of the others in the room. The list of transgressions committed by the mysterious baldheaded man and his allies continued to grow; only an hour ago it had been learned that another Orka agent in Spain had been seriously wounded by a bomb blast. His condition was guarded. Logan knew he wouldn't stop till each act was avenged. Achmed's death, the attack on Josh Leighman, Tate Osgood in Spain, and his own particular problems—four direct attacks that indirectly touched all Orka agents.

"Let's don't any of us give up," Allen said encouragingly.

"Personally, I don't think 'giving up' has anything to do with the situation, Allen. An unknown group or individual has cut quite a swath through the ranks of our organization, and we haven't a clue as to who is responsible."

"We still haven't heard from all our sources."

"That's all well and good, but just how much time do we have? With all three conferences cranking up within a few days of each other, we're going to be busy as hell. Have other agencies been apprised of the facts?"

Allen nodded. "A full disclosure has been filed with each one. They've responded by offering any assistance we might need."

"I seriously doubt we need to go that far," Logan retorted, bringing a smile of amusement to Allen's lips. The agencies were viciously competitive and never lost a chance to take potshots at each other. "Have you decided on the schedule yet?"

"You and Cal will cover the conference in Florida. McDonald will be joining you in a couple of days. Any questions?"

"When do you want us in place?"

"I think at least four days before the conference begins should be sufficient. Each of you will be able to secure gardening or maintenance positions before the big day. That way, you'll have access to the building proper and the grounds."

"That shouldn't be any problem. Is the hotel a chain or privately owned?"

"Privately owned, but they'll cooperate. They're not in the least anxious for any type of unpleasant publicity. Ask for Sam Levine when you get there."

"How much time do we have before we go south?"

"Sorry, friend. Three days—that's the best I

could come up with. If we knew who we were fighting, then it could all be handled differently. As it is, it's like fighting some mysterious disease—with no idea what it is or how it gets started."

"Oh, really?" Logan asked mockingly.

Allen looked chagrined. "Sorry."

Logan threw a hand. "Don't apologize. This thing's gotten to all of us." He got to his feet. "Am I through here?"

Allen also rose. "Don't see why not. Headed anyplace special?"

"The Crescent City has a rather strange pull these days. Since I can't seem to get the sound of jazz out of my head, I suppose I'll just have to go down there."

"Best damned idea you've had in years, Gant. Matter of fact . . . think I'll try a little of that jazz myself. Any objections?"

A grin split Logan's rough features. "Not at all—be glad of the company."

Hubie Fontenot came through the door of the small office in his usual rush. He was of medium height, nicely built, and blond. At the moment the huge white apron he wore when cooking was in place, with a large pink stain marring the otherwise pristine whiteness. "Caroline isn't coming in today—sick, or something."

204

"Don't worry, Hubie, we'll make out," Skylar assured him, looking up from where she was working on the restaurant's books. Hubie lived in a continual ulcerous frazzle. The slightest upheaval saw the busboy heading for the closest drugstore to lay in a large supply of Mylanta. He was one-third owner of the restaurant, and Skylar and Joey—the other partner—were well aware that Hubie was the most important part of the business. He was one of three chefs and was fast developing a reputation for himself and his creole cuisine.

"Why aren't people reliable, Sky?" He began to pace, a practice that drove Skylar up the wall.

"Most people are, Hubie. Caroline is still painfully young. She hasn't yet learned the importance of reliability."

"She's learned the importance of eating, hasn't she?" he returned. "Hasn't it occurred to her that if she doesn't work, she doesn't get money?"

"Apparently it hasn't, dear, or she would have her little tush out there in a couple of hours, beaming dazzling smiles of welcome upon our customers. But don't worry, I'll take care of it." Poor dear, she silently sympathized with him. He was so much in love with the irresponsible young Caroline, it was pathetic.

"I know you will. But you have other duties, Sky. We pay Caroline a very good salary. You'd think she would do us the courtesy of trying to perform her duties as is expected of her."

Skylar mentally shuddered as her partner became more and more wound up. Once he reached that particular stage, there was nothing to do but let him get it off his chest.

"When are you going to get up nerve enough to ask Caroline out, Hubie?"

He shot her a quick, haughty look, then continued his pacing.

"Don't give me that go-to-hell look, Hubie. If you weren't such a coward, you would have to spend absolutely thousands of dollars on Mylanta. You could let your ulcer take a long vacation by letting Caroline *know* how you feel, rather than acting like a grouchy bear all the time."

"She thinks I'm too old for her," he said distantly.

"Did she tell you that?"

"Certainly not."

"Then may one ask how you arrived at such an idiotic conclusion? Did you perhaps consult your crystal ball? The one with the three-inch crack in it?"

"How do you do it?" Hubie looked at her.

"Do what?"

"Always manage to make me laugh. I come to you when I'm low, and in minutes you have me laughing. It's a gift—a very wonderful gift you possess, Sky. By the way, when is that mysterious houseguest of yours coming back?"

"Er . . . I'm not sure," Skylar murmured, not wanting to discuss Logan with anyone. She was positively terrified of letting something slip that would cause harm to come to him.

"Don't worry, honey." Hubie walked behind the desk and patted her shoulder as he went by. "You know Joey and I would never say or do anything to hurt you."

She smiled. "I know. And I honestly do wish I could tell you something more, but I can't."

"Don't worry." Hubie grinned. "What you 'can't' or 'won't' tell us, we found out when we dragged Francine in here and blackmailed her into filling us in on what was going on. Must say, honey, those apartments you live in are tops for excitement."

"If you dare say one word about Logan," Skylar threatened him, "I'll personally cut your throat."

"Ahh, such kind words." He tapped his chest with a fist. "All that confidence you have in your friends really warms my heart."

"Friends and warm hearts have nothing to

207

do with it, Hubie. We're talking life-and-death situations here. And I'm not kidding."

"Mmmm. Maybe we shouldn't have pressed Francine so hard. What if your boyfriend's enemies come after your two partners?" he teased.

"You're impossible."

"True, but I'm one hell of a chef. I'm too old for her, you know."

"Only in your mind," Skylar told him, having not the slightest problem following his conversation. The mention of Logan's name had merely sidetracked him, not deterred him in the least from the subject of the lovely Caroline.

"The mind can be a very difficult thing to get around."

Skylar laid down her pencil, then leaned back in her chair and stared at her friend. "Hubie, may I give you some advice?"

"Certainly."

"Why on earth don't you at least ask the girl out on a date? Do you realize we've been having this same conversation approximately once a week for over a year now? In my opinion you've thought about it long enough. For God's sake, man. *Do something!*"

For several minutes Hubie continued his pacing. Finally he stopped. With his hands clasped behind his back he turned and stared at Skylar. "Flowers, I think. Red or yellow roses?"

"Flowers?" she asked. Goodness. He really was going to get into the swing of things. "Frankly, I prefer yellow ones."

"Good. I'll take care of it now." Without further discussion he walked over to the desk, picked up the phone, and placed the order.

Skylar sat back smiling. Well, what the hell? she thought. At least he wasn't driving her up the wall with that damned pacing.

At ten forty-five Skylar put the ledgers away, then went to the small powder room off the office and freshened her makeup. Hostessing wasn't her favorite job, but since she and the two men took turns at doing whatever came up, she didn't complain.

By eleven-ten a steady stream of customers had begun, and she'd even had three parties call and make reservations. Joey, who took care of the small, discreet bar to the left of the foyer, groaned when he came in and she handed him the three slips.

"Will you please tell me why anybody would want to make reservations for lunch? It's too damned early to do any serious talking."

Skylar laughed at the tall blond, even though she agreed with him. Luncheon reservations always created more problems than they were worth—unless it happened to be a very large party.

"Unfortunately, Joseph," she said to him, "We have to take the good with the bad."

"By the way." He grinned mischievously at her. "Guess who called you a while ago. While you were making the bank deposit."

Skylar's face turned white as a sheet. "Who?"

"Auntie Katherine."

"And?" She knew there had to be more, he was looking entirely too smug.

"She's coming to lunch. Then she's going to spend the night in town and expects you to dine with her this evening. Seems it's time for the meeting of the board for the hospital and the bank."

"Ahhh . . . her board meetings. I'd forgotten."

Joey laughed. "I thought as much, but I didn't dare say it for fear the next time she saw me, she'd whack hell out of me with that cane she carries."

Skylar chuckled. Due to her bluntness and sharp tongue, Katherine Damler had quite a reputation among her niece's friends. They liked the older woman, but every one of them was in awe of her. "Perhaps she'll insist you join her for lunch."

"Now, look, Sky," Joey began, "the last time

I ate with that old lady, all she talked about was the Civil War."

"Really?" she asked with feigned sweetness, struggling not to laugh. "I sincerely hope you didn't disappoint her by not showing the proper interest."

Joey rolled his eyes upward. "I tried, kid, I really did. But about all I know about that period in history is that there was a war."

"Mmmm. Well,"—she sighed—"I can assure you Aunt Katherine won't let that little oversight go unattended."

"What's that suppose to mean?" Joey asked alertly.

"Why, Joseph," Skylar softly exclaimed. "Where's your sporting blood? Just suffice it to say, Auntie Katherine will take care of the matter."

"No wonder you and that old lady get along so well together. You're just like her," he complained.

"Thank you, sir." She dipped her head grandly. "Aunt Katherine is very dear to me."

Later, as Skylar ushered diners to various tables, she smiled and was pleasant, but her mind was on the imminent appearance of her relative. She couldn't help but wonder how Katherine would have reacted to Logan.

What do you mean *would have* reacted? a small voice asked her. You're talking like the

211

man is never coming . . . as if he's dead or something.

Skylar couldn't explain the slip. Logan had promised to return, and she had no reason to doubt he would keep his word. . . .

It hit her then, with the thrust of a cannonball landing in the middle of her chest; Logan might die on his assignment, and there was nothing at all she could do to stop it!

With legs trembling like matchsticks, she made her way back to the antique sideboard that served as a counter, slipped behind it, and edged her hips against the tall stool. Her face felt warm, as if she'd been standing next to a hot fireplace. Her heartbeat had accelerated to an incredible rate, leaving her breathless and shaking. The words *Logan might die* kept running through her mind.

"Skylar," Joey said, "a Mrs. Martin just called, she's running a little late, but will be shortly joining the party at table number six. Would you mind tell— Skylar? What on earth's wrong?" He came around the barrier of dark, polished wood, his face full of concern. He leaned down in front of her, his back shielding her from any curious eye that might happen to be looking her way. "Honey? Has something happened to Aunt Katherine?"

Skylar shook her head, not sure her voice was working, she was shaking so badly. "I—I think I must b-be coming down with something," she finally managed. She placed a hand on Joey's arm and squeezed it. "Don't worry, I'll be fine. I'm sure Aunt Katherine will have something in her great store of home remedies that will have me in tip top shape in mere hours."

"You sure?"

"Positive. Now," she forced herself to smile as she pushed herself upright. Her hands became busy, smoothing the green silk skirt over her hips and patting at the collar of the matching blouse. "If we don't get back to work, that slave driver in the kitchen will come after us with the meat cleaver."

"Never mind his meat cleaver." Joey frowned. For a while, several years ago, he had been head over heels in love with Skylar. Except for one particular evening, when several of them were out together, and he had too much to drink and revealed his feelings to her, they had maintained a sort of brother-and-sister relationship. "Are you sure you're okay?"

"Positive, Joey. Besides which, I must— Well, Joey my friend, you can start worrying. I'll bet you five dollars my darling aunt has brought you some books on the Civil War."

He turned and followed her gaze to the entrance. Tiny, white-haired Katherine Damler, elegant in a rose silk suit, complete with hat and gloves, was waiting with all the dignity of a queen—ebony cane in hand—to be shown to her table.

Skylar hurried forward, a smile on her face. "Aunt Katherine," she said when she reached the older woman. She hugged the fragile body and pressed her smooth cheek against Katherine's warm, gently lined one. "It's so good to see you."

"Skylar dear." Katherine held her at arm's length, her clear green eyes running carefully over her only relation. "You've lost weight, and there's no color in your cheeks. What's going on with you?"

"Nothing's going on with me, Aunt Katherine, except work," Skylar assured her. "Business is great. It keeps us all busy."

About that time Joey, who'd been waiting for the two of them to get their private greetings done with, stepped forward. "Aunt Katherine." He smiled, taking her small, veined hand in his. "It's a pleasure to see you. You're looking especially lovely today."

"Thank you, Joseph." Katherine nodded regally. "Your courtliness is refreshing—as always. Are you still wasting your talents tending bar?"

The fact that Joey was one-third owner of the restaurant mattered little to Katherine.

She still considered him to be wasting an enormous potential by not joining the world of banking, law, or securities.

"Still hanging in there, Aunt Katherine. I have decided to take a couple of business courses this fall, though," he said, not adding that he was doing so in order to better manage the restaurant. Skylar kept books well, Hubie cooked well, but neither had a head for business. That left the burden on Joey's shoulders.

"Wonderful." The tiny woman beamed. "I knew my urgings wouldn't go unnoticed. However, I should think you'd take a course in history. I distinctly remember how poorly informed you were on *the war*."

"The war?" he was foolish and forgetful enough to ask.

He was regarded archly. "My dear young man. The Civil War was and is *the war*. Now, would one or both of you please show me to my table? And, Skylar, please see that Bernard is taken care of. He'd rather starve than join me."

"Bernard believes in the strict observance of proprieties," Skylar told her aunt as Joey offered Katherine his arm. He escorted her to a special table, kept available for family or close friends, that looked out onto the brick patio, where tubs of plants and hanging baskets added their own special touch to the overall charm of the restaurant.

"That's all well and good, but what would it hurt for the darn man to sit at the same table with me?"

"Nothing, Aunt Katherine—as far as you're concerned. But for Bernard, it would be a sacrilege. He's very devoted to you, you know."

"I suppose so," Katherine murmured. "Though it does make it difficult when we're out most of the day. Why, most times I put off eating because I know he wouldn't dream of joining me, and he won't detain me by having me wait for him. It gets to be downright annoying."

Skylar's resigned gaze met Joey's amused one. "Will you please see to Bernard? He might enjoy eating in the bar."

"Good idea. I'll take care of it. Excuse me, Aunt Katherine, while I take of your chauffeur. We'll chat some more before you leave."

"Thank you, Joseph." She watched him walk away. "He's such a nice young man, Skylar. You're very fortunate in your choice of business partners. Hubert and Joseph are honest men. That's a rarity these days."

"I'm sure it is." Skylar took a menu from the waitress, then raised the glass of water to her lips. "Thank you, Susie. Would you please bring my aunt a very light bourbon and water? Then, in approximately twenty minutes, you may bring her a bowl of clear soup. I'll have a small salad and ice tea."

"Yes, ma'am," Susie agreed, clearly terrified of the tiny but imposing figure of Aunt Katherine. This was her first time to wait on the old lady, she was thinking, and she wanted everything to be just right. She'd heard stories from some of the other girls who'd been at Hubie's longer than she had, about how outspoken the old woman was.

The conversation, as soon as Susie was away from the table, began immediately. It had been over three weeks since Skylar had seen her aunt, and there was all kinds of gossip to catch up on.

"The garden guild has asked me to let them show the house during the Christmas tour this year," Katherine announced. Her home, Amsley, while not a large, imposing structure, was a very well preserved example of the creole cottage style of architecture. It was white, with long green shutters at the windows and doors. It was raised several feet off the ground, to accommodate the floods of the era during which it was built. A spacious verandah ran across the front, with wide cypress steps leading down to the four-acre grounds surrounding it. The house had been built in the middle eighteen hundreds by Katherine's grandfather for his bride, when he was a young man. Because he was youngest of four sons, his life-style was somewhat more modest than that of his eldest brother, who inherited the two-storied plantation home.

Susie returned with Katherine's bourbon and water, then fled immediately following the older woman's polite "Thank you."

"Are you going to let them?"

"After their allowing all those candles to drip wax on my floors, I seriously doubt it."

"You certainly have a point there," Skylar agreed. The year before, she'd gone and helped her aunt and Madeline, Katherine's housekeeper, get ready for the tour. Not a single lady from the guild had shown up to help, nor did they offer any help with cleanup afterward. "I think I'd simply tell them that because of the shabby way they treated you last year, your home will not be available to them this year."

Katherine smiled. "It's so nice when you agree with me, dear. But then, we almost always agree on things, don't we?"

"Yes, we do. By the way, how is Colonel Merriweather?"

"Like a sore-tailed cat. Can you believe he actually had the nerve to come calling last week?"

"What did you do?"

"Threatened to take Papa's horsewhip to him if he didn't get off my property."

"But, Aunt Katherine," Skylar tried to reason with her. "The poor colonel. Don't you think it's time the two of you buried the hatchet? After all, it's been nearly twenty years or better since you jilted him. And you've known each other all your lives. Doesn't that count for something?"

"It does not, and it'll be twenty more before I let that snake in my house. I caught him kissing another woman only two days before we were to be married, Skylar. Two days! How can he expect me to forgive such deceit as that?"

"Having listened to your stories of the Widow Larson, I think it's very possible that she was the one doing the kissing."

"Then he should have been more careful of who he had conversations with."

"Won't you even read one of his letters? I know he faithfully writes to you twice a week. In all these years have you read any of the letters?"

A slight blush touched Katherine's cheek. She raised her chin in the air. "One or two. There was nothing of importance in them. For the life of me I can't figure out why the old fool keeps sending them."

"He must still love you. Or maybe it's a matter of pride. You know, you aren't the only one allowed that privilege."

Green eyes exactly like her own steadily regarded her across the table. "You sound as if you're on his side."

"I'm on your side, dear. But I do wish you would be just a bit kinder to the poor man, Aunt Katherine. Would you consider it—for my sake?"

A short silence ensued, during which Katherine sipped contentedly at her bourbon. "If it will make you happy, then I'll let the old fool speak his piece. But *only* at my convenience," she tacked on.

"Well, I should think so," Skylar said soothingly. "After all, he is in the wrong. Now that we've got that all settled, I feel better. So tell me, what's on the agenda of the board meeting for the bank and the hospital? Anything spicy?"

"Dull as dishwater. You know, Skylar dear, old people are boring. Please don't let me get that way when I get old. It's positively humiliating. At any rate, the bank will declare its usual dividend, name another chairman in Walter's place, and that's it. The hospital is getting geared up for its annual fund drive, and the usual piddling things that crop up in a meeting. The only reason I even bothered

220

coming in was to see you. I'd begun to think you'd forgotten me."

Skylar reached across the table for Katherine's hand. "I'm sorry. Lately I've had some very peculiar things happening in my life, Aunt Katherine. I'm not ready to talk about them at the moment, but one day soon I promise to drive out and tell you everything."

"Does it involve a man?"

"Yes. Why?"

"Well . . ." Katherine took a deep breath, then gently smiled at her niece. "A very tall, very broad-shouldered man with a very striking face has been speaking with Joey. They've been gesturing and looking at our table. Now that same man is headed this way."

Skylar sat frozen. Very tall . . . very broad shouldered . . . very striking face . . . that could only mean one man: Logan. She didn't turn around to greet him. She couldn't, her mind wouldn't accept the signal that her body was suppose to move. His presence drew nearer . . . and nearer. When he was beside the table, she felt the pressure of his wide hand drop to her shoulder.

"Hello, Skylar."

She raised her head, her green eyes luminous with unshed tears. She was terribly afraid her heart was as open to his probing gaze as her face. Her lips quivered when she made the superhuman effort of trying to will them into a facsimile of a smile.

His blue eyes feasted hungrily on her, touching each visible part of her and storing it in his memory.

"L-Logan," she whispered. "Hello."

When it looked as though she was incapable of saying another word, Logan took Katherine's hand in his own. "I'm Logan Gant."

"Katherine Damler, Skylar's great-aunt."

"A pleasure meeting you, Mrs. Damler. Remind me someday to tell a very funny story about a man in a wheelchair. Now I see where Skylar gets her beauty and, quite likely, her sense of humor. She looks remarkably like you."

"How kind of you to say so, Mr. Logan." She gestured to a chair. "Please, will you join us?"

He sat down, his eyes going back to the still-shaken Skylar. "I hope you don't have plans for dinner this evening."

"I don't," she said softly.

"Good. I have the perfect thing in mind."

"How delightful," Katherine chimed in, very alert to the near-traumatized state of her niece. So he was responsible for the "peculiar things" happening in her life . . . interesting. "I like a man of decision, Logan, very much. I'm also a student of the Civil War. Any comment?"

Logan regarded Katherine Damler for several amused seconds, a suspicious twinkle in his blue eyes. As she grew older, Skylar would look exactly like her aunt. That pleased him. "I think it was the war of wars. Shall we discuss it sometime?"

CHAPTER TWELVE

Skylar and Logan lay in bed in the middle of the afternoon. Skylar felt positively wicked at enjoying such wanton pleasure in the daytime.

"Where were you last night, Ms. Dennis? I called three different times and was never able to get you." His lips closed like velvet around a turgid nipple, drawing, sucking . . . wave after wave of incredible pleasure washing over her.

"Ohhh." Skylar closed her eyes tightly, her fingers molding themselves to the shape of his head and pressing him closer . . . closer to her. "How can you expect me to answer you?" She gasped.

"Because," Logan said slowly, licking his way to the other breast and the waiting tip, "I'm selfish enough to want to know every single thing about you. I want to know who you were with . . . what you did."

"Sounds mighty one way to me, Mr. Gant."

she murmured, then felt the air rushing from her lungs when his hands touched the tops of her thighs and the sensitive quick of her being. They swept on, reacquainting themselves with each dip and line of her body.

"You've been on my mind almost the entire time we've been apart," he whispered. "I'd be looking at a face on the screen, when suddenly that same face would become astonishingly familiar . . . ugly, cruel features would be miraculously softened and smoothed into beautiful ones . . . I'd blink my eyes to clear my head, then presto! Your face would be smiling back at me, with that sexy little grin pulling at your lips."

Skylar smiled. "Oh, my. Keep that up, and I do believe you will turn my head."

He moved over her, his lips hovering achingly close to hers. "I want to turn your head, sweetheart. I want you to become so addicted to me, you can't even begin to think of not having me in your life." His mouth crushed hers, taking her lips roughly in a kiss that awakened a deep, dark, primitive force within Skylar, drawing from her a response that equaled his assaulting mouth.

While their mouths were joined, Logan claimed her in that other way that sent numerous infinitesimal shudders of desire spreading out over the surface of her body like the ever-widening circles going out from the intrusion of a tiny pebble suddenly dropped into a peaceful lake.

They climbed the craggy slopes of passion, reveling in the winds of desire buffeting the vulnerable fringes of their emotions. On and on they climbed, thinking they were reaching the summit in an unduly short time, only to learn that it was not to be . . . yet. When they did scale the last outcropping of ecstasy, the descent into the valley below left them exhausted, their bodies filmed with perspiration.

Later, while Logan was making some phone calls, Skylar was in the shower, reliving those moments of lovemaking in her mind. It had been different, yet the exact nature of the difference eluded her. Sensitivity for her feelings and concern for her enjoyment had, as before, dominated Logan's actions. Yet he'd instilled a sense of . . . of what?

Skylar reached for the faucet and turned off the pulsating stream of water, then pushed back the door and stepped out. As her hand went out and brought the large towel to her body, she became still, a curious blend of emotions gathering in her eyes. The difference she was looking for had been the sense of desperation she'd felt in Logan.

She couldn't define any actual difference in

227

his lovemaking, yet it was there. What was it? she wondered.

That question still hung heavy on her mind when she entered the kitchen some time later. Logan was still talking, and from what he was saying, she could readily tell it was business-related. That fact alone was enough to put a damper on the closeness they'd shared only a short time ago.

The petulant slant of her lips wasn't lost to Logan a few minutes later as he replaced the receiver and turned to watch Skylar busily putting together a salad.

"Something on your mind?" he asked alertly. His tall, powerful body tensed. He was waiting for her response like a man about to be sentenced.

Skylar glanced up at him. The expression in his eyes halted the curt reply already forming on her lips. She wondered, however, if that was wise. Sooner or later they were going to be forced to discuss their growing feelings for each other.

"Are you going to have to leave this evening?" The question was eons from what she really wanted to say to him, yet the thought of his leaving, to face God only knew what kind of monsters, had tempered her words.

Logan leaned one black-clad shoulder against the wall, his arms crossed over his chest. "It will be several days before I'll be leaving. Does that news make you happy or sad?"

She faced him, a piece of lettuce in each hand. "Now what do you think, Logan Gant?"

He tipped his head to one side and smiled at her. "I think it has to make you as happy as it does me."

"Enough said. So." She made a huge effort to douse the tears that had suddenly welled to life in her eyes. "As soon as I get this darn salad finished, let's sit down and make some plans. How does that grab you?"

"In the most vulnerable spot of all, Ms. Dennis," he teased. He walked over to her. His hands clasped her head and turned her to him. He dropped a quick, hard kiss on her startled but very willing lips, then took down two mugs and fixed coffee for each of them. "And just to let you know that if you're thinking I'm vulnerable only in one spot where you're concerned, I'll have you know I was referring to my heart," he said smugly.

"Ah-ha," Skylar hooted. "Some heart."

She finished the salad and put it in the refrigerator for later, then wiped off her hands and sat down at the table. "Do you realize we seldom sit in my"—she glowered at him in mock anger—"beautifully decorated living room?"

Without another word Logan rose to his full height. He took a couple of steps to her side, plucked her from the chair, and strode from the room. He didn't stop till he was in front of the sofa, where he dropped her onto the plump cushions. His much heavier body followed close behind.

He quickly reached down and removed her shoes and his, then plunked her feet on the coffee table, following suit with his own only seconds later. One arm shot out and caught Skylar by the arm and pulled her over till she was firmly tucked against his ribs; his other arm dropped behind her head, his palm clasping her shoulder.

"How do you like that?" he asked, looking down his generous nose at her.

"Impressive," Skylar answered solemnly, "very impressive. I like a man of decision. You forgot only one thing."

Logan frowned. "What's that?"

"My pad and pen. There was a pad and pen lying on the table. I was about to use it to jot down the plans we were going to make for the time we have together."

"Who needs pads and pencils?" Logan sighed contentedly. He wiggled his toes, managing to rake one down the bottom of Skylar's foot. She squealed and the fight was on.

It took only a moment or two for Logan to

subdue his attacker. The punishment was a kiss, to which the villan eagerly responded. "What happened to that little wildcat I was just holding in my arms, the one who called me a pig with a huge snout?" he demanded to know.

"You still do have a huge snout, but I suppose you aren't that much of a pig." She knew defeat had never been so sweet.

"Ha!" he continued, both her wrists imprisoned in his large hands and raised over her head. She was lying on the sofa, her legs caught and held between his hard thighs. "Do you promise never to call me ugly names again—even when I tickle your feet? And do you promise to say very nice things about my handsome nose—even when I tickle your feet?"

"No!" Skylar exclaimed. "Never."

"Ahh, well." He shook his head. "In that case." He transferred both wrists to one hand, then reached to the other side of him and grabbed a slim foot.

Skylar began calling him all sorts of names and squirmed for dear life.

Logan merely grinned and began tickling her foot.

The battle was in full swing when there was an imperious knock on the door.

They froze.

A guarded expression slipped like a mask over Logan's face. "From the way that sounded, must be a damned giant." He sat Skylar aside, then got to his feet and shot out of the room incredibly fast for such a large man. He returned in seconds, the flash of metal lying flat against his palm. "Get in the hall, honey, and stay there till we know who this is."

A gun. She'd actually seen a gun in his hand. Dear Lord!

Skylar stumbled upright, fear gripping her stomach. "Logan?" The one word held a wealth of meaning. It was a plea to him to restore the world the way it was before the sound at the door, to reassure her somehow that this wasn't the way he lived. No human being—or a married couple—could possibly stand the pressure.

The knock came again—just as loud.

"Do as I told you." Skylar stared incredulously at him, as if seeing him change before her very eyes. The five words were spoken in a voice she had never heard Logan use. It shocked her. It was cold, devoid of feeling. The man across the room from her was a stranger. It simply wasn't possible for it to be coming from the same gentle person who had made love to her a while ago. The overall change was incredible.

His eyes were narrowed slits of cold, emotionless blue ice. The mouth that had evoked such passion in her was now a rigid slash, devoid of feeling. It simply wasn't possible.

But it is, her conscience told her. It is, Skylar, and you're doing nothing but fooling yourself if you think otherwise. You started out fine. You vowed never to become involved with another man even remotely connected to law enforcement.

Skylar moved slowly backward to the door leading into the hall. She knew she'd made herself a lot of promises, but Logan was different.

Please, her weary conscience said mockingly. Not only have you gone and done the very thing you swore not to do, you've picked a man whose career is twenty times more dangerous than Tim's ever was. The only difference is, Tim was a show-off and it got him killed. Logan, on the other hand, is sensible enough to exercise caution. Which probably means, he'll get his by having a bomb tossed into his car . . . or having his house blown up. Either way, it doesn't leave you a very pleasant choice, does it?

Logan reached out for the doorknob. He

stood to one side, his body poised, his hand tight on the knob, and threw open the door.

Katherine Damler reared back instinctively when the door opened so abruptly. Bernard, who was standing slightly behind her, had an equally puzzled expression on his face as they stared at Logan.

"I—I . . . Good evening, Logan," Katherine said faintly, clearly rattled by his actions. "Is my niece in?"

Logan took a deep breath, then exhaled noisily. He clasped the back of his neck with one hand, clearly at a disadvantage for one of the few times in his life. "Hello, Katherine . . . Bernard." He stepped aside. "Come in . . . please. Skylar's inside."

"Aunt Katherine. What a pleasant surprise," Skylar came forward, smiling. "Do come in. Bernard?" She looked questioningly at the older man still standing in the corridor outside her front door.

"No thanks." he tipped his dark cloth cap to her. "I'll just wait out here till Miz Damler's ready." He turned and walked away, leaving Logan no choice but to close the door.

Katherine stood in the center of the room, leaning more heavily than usual on her cane. She shivered, feeling the tension hovering in the room like a heavy fog. She looked from

Skylar to Logan. "Something's wrong, isn't it?"

Skylar chuckled and caught her hand. "I'm sorry, Aunt Katherine, I suppose I should have told you this afternoon, but I didn't want to worry you."

"Told me what?"

Logan walked over and slipped an arm around Skylar's waist. "Annoying phone calls," he said simply. "They're about to drive her nuts. All during the night . . . the minute she sets foot into the apartment. I'm of the opinion it's someone who can see her come and go."

"I see." Katherine nodded her tiny white head. "You thought perhaps they'd gotten brave enough to annoy her in person?"

He shrugged. "Something like that. I assume you used that"—nodding toward her cane—"to knock with?"

"Yes. It saves my knuckles."

"It sounded like a twelve-foot giant was on the other side of the door," he said consolingly. "Skylar had gotten only one call since we got here, so I suppose I overreacted. Sorry if we upset you."

"Oh, no." Katherine patted his arm. "I'm just delighted my niece has someone as determined as you to look after her. A woman living alone these days is fair game for all the oddballs floating around."

Skylar guided her to a wing-backed chair. "Sit here, Aunt Katherine."

"Thank you, dear. My, this is a comfortable chair." She smiled as she sank back against the tall back. "So big too. Logan, you should take this as your very own. It appears to be made for a man of your stature. Now. The reason I dropped by was to see if you could come to Amsley for dinner tomorrow evening. I could have phoned, but"—she lifted her hands expressively—"I didn't."

Logan and Skylar exchanged inquiring glances. "I'm free," he said, "how about you?"

"Oh, I think I can get off," Skylar answered. "Why don't we come early so I can take Logan through the house and over the grounds, Aunt Katherine?"

"Sounds like a splendid idea. If he's interested in fishing, he might like to wet a hook or two. Even though the evenings are beginning to get cool, the bass are biting nicely. Bernard keeps us well supplied. Now that we've taken care of that little matter, I think I'd better be on my way."

She extended a hand toward Logan. "If you'll help me out of this chair, that is. Being of diminutive size has it's drawbacks, young man." He helped her to her feet, then joined

Skylar in seeing her into Bernard's capable hands.

Once the two of them were back inside the apartment, there seemed to be no words to explain, to make better, to change, what had happened. After a tense few minutes of studiously avoiding looking at Logan, Skylar excused herself and went to her bedroom.

Logan wanted to go after her. He even took a faltering step or two, then stopped. What the hell! She needed the time alone, and if he were honest with himself, so did he. Without giving himself time to change his mind, he walked over to the door, opened it, and stepped out into the corridor. Perhaps a walk would help him think better.

A park three blocks down the street drew Logan's interest, and he was soon seated in a large swing beneath two spreading oak trees, his mind and thoughts taken over with the past and its hellishly ironic resemblance to the present.

There in the night, with the shadows of the trees protecting him from prying eyes, he gave full vent to his thoughts and memories. The fragile loveliness of Iseult swam before the windows of his mind, teasing him with her shy smile. He saw them swimming in the cool stream, saw them at the ranch in Colorado, rolling in the snow like two kids.

She'd told him then . . . as he'd rolled her over on top of him. He'd caught the edges of her wool cap and pulled them over her face.

"Is that anyway to treat the mother of your child, Gant?"

Logan remembered his stunned, trancelike reaction to her announcement. Once he regained a small measure of self-control, he'd crushed her to him, both of them damp with snow, but feeling nothing but incredible, unbelievable happiness. He, Logan Gant—a name given him by a stranger after he'd been found abandoned as an infant—was to be a father.

Their happiness had been complete. Iseult was an artist; her paintings of wildflowers and landscapes, were eagerly sought by many. Logan remembered how proud he'd been of her when she'd had her first show. God! It seemed so long ago . . . so recent. A sudden shiver shook his large frame. It was as if he could reach out and touch Iseult . . . in fact he did reach out—to nothing . . . nothing.

He closed his eyes defeatedly, then thought of the ranch. He'd borrowed everything he could get his hands on in his early twenties. He'd invested every cent in the market. Through some weird stroke of fate he had a knack for picking the right ones. Later, when Iseult came into his life—became his wife—

238

she'd stood on the native stone terrace that banked the rear of the house, the snow gently falling about her, and predicted that when summer came, she could sun the baby on the terrace.

Tears fell readily from Logan's eyes as he remembered how he'd held her to him, his large hands clasped protectively over the slight bulge in her stomach. His son. His son.

They'd both left him three days later. . . . Iseult met a friend in town for lunch. They left the restaurant laughing and talking. Iseult stepped off the curb without looking.

Logan raised a hand and wiped a rough hand over his eyes. God! The poor bastard who hit her had been pathetic, he remembered. He'd stood before Logan, wringing his hands, shaking his head back and forth. Logan had walked away from him, unable to cope with the death, much less console the driver of the car.

He took a vow, standing in the same spot on the terrace where Iseult had stood. He vowed no woman would ever replace her in his heart, in his life. Afterward, he'd hired a couple to look after the ranch and gone with Orka. From there on, the agency became his life . . . till Skylar. Now he had a decision to make.

But what if he were to lose her as he'd lost

Iseult? he asked himself. What then? Without blinking an eye Logan accepted the answer to that question. It was simple, really. He knew without a single doubt he wouldn't want to live.

So where does that leave you, Logan Gant? You saw the repulsion in Skylar's eyes a while ago when she watched you become the Logan Gant who's stayed alive all these years by training, instinct, and by outwitting your adversaries. You can't stop till you've avenged Achmed's death, yet you quite probably run the awesome risk of losing the woman you never thought you'd find. You loved Iseult with that youthful abandon that's so exhausting. With Skylar it's the complete thing—the one chance that comes in a lifetime.

He had no ready answers for the questions his conscience had posed. It seemed that either way he would lose. If he continued with Orka, he would lose Skylar. If he left Orka and ignored the scum responsible for Achmed's death, he would lose his pride and his self-respect.

The joggers and late-night walkers had long since left the track when the tall, quiet man left his lonely vigil beneath the spreading oaks, no more comfortable with what his thoughts had revealed than when he'd first sought solace in the dark shadows.

* * *

Skylar was roused from her fitful slumber by the shifting of the bed. "Logan?" she asked, startled, brushing back a lazy tendril of hair that had fallen across her forehead.

A warm hand slipped to the curve of her hip. "Go back to sleep, honey. It's way past midnight."

"Are you coming to bed?"

"Yes," he said tiredly, "I'm coming."

She turned onto her back, watching the shadowy outline of him as he undressed, then got into the bed. Yet she made no attempt to touch him, nor he her. "Where have you been?" she whispered. For some strange reason it seemed terribly urgent that she whisper. As if some silent specter . . . some ghost . . . walked the edge of darkness within the room, listening to what they had to say to each other.

"I went to the park and sat in one of those old-fashioned swings under the oak trees. It's a very peaceful place."

"That park was built on the land that was once part of a plantation. The ground beneath those two particular oaks you're talking about, where the swings are located, is said to be haunted."

Again Logan felt an inexplicable shiver sweep his body from head to foot.

"Logan? Are you cold?" Skylar asked. She reached out and touched him then. He felt warm. When she went to pull her hand away, it was caught and held.

"Go on with your story, honey."

"I suppose it sounds silly to some people, but I've always felt sad when I thought about it and the people involved. Seems there was this family of immense wealth. There were several children, all early teens to early twenties. The war came, and with it the usual sadness and hardships. This family didn't fare too badly, however. The father was smart enough to put gold on deposit in banks in San Francisco and London. At any rate, the next-to-the-youngest daughter, the father's favorite, had helped her mother nurse the soldiers during the war. She met and fell in love with a Yankee captain. After the war he came back to New Orleans. He asked for her hand, and her father refused."

"Sounds like the typical response," Logan murmured. "Did they run away? Which is also typical."

Skylar hit him playfully on the shoulder. "Spoilsport. There isn't a romantic bone in your overgrown body, Logan Gant."

"If I say I'm very sorry, will you please tell me the rest of the story?" he teased her. He reached for her then, and pulled her into his arms.

Her arm touched the spot where he'd been shot. "I'm sorry," she said quickly. "It's healing so quickly, I sometimes forget about it."

"Good," he told her. "And it *is* almost well. There's barely any soreness left. But you're not off the hook, Ms. Dennis. I want to know what happened to your young lovers."

Skylar sighed. "All right, but only if you promise not to laugh."

"I promise," he said solemnly.

"When the father turned down the young man's proposal, the lovers were devastated. They made plans to elope, plans that were immediately carried to the father's ear by a devoted servant. A substitute was found to replace the daughter for the appointed time. The father also planned to have the young man killed. Unfortunately, the young woman hired to replace the daughter found she couldn't go through with the deception, and told the daughter. They swapped places, and that evening, when the couple were making their escape, three hired gunmen came thundering after them. The captain fought gallantly, but he was no match for three. In the ensuing skirmish it was the girl who was accidentally killed. The Yankee captain was severely wounded, but survived. The tragedy

243

happened beneath those two trees where you were sitting tonight. It's said the young captain haunts the shadows, tears of sadness streaming down his handsome face as he mourns the death of his darling."

CHAPTER THIRTEEN

Skylar stared disbelievingly at the navy-blue Mercedes parked beside her battered VW. "It's haughty, stuck up, and a disgrace," she declared with a certain dignity that instantly made Logan think of Katherine Damler.

Logan bent and patted the rear fender of the atrocious little car. "Er . . . please excuse me. No harm meant." He straightened, looking as solemn as a judge.

"You are an ass!" she hissed, really throwing herself into the exchange. "Just for good measure I think I'll have Aunt Katherine loan me Grandfather Latimer's horsewhip. That should take care of that smart mouth of yours."

"That's right, ladies." He smiled past her. "You heard her. Abuse. Plain and simple. People won't believe it when I try to tell them how abused I am."

"You poor man," a feminine voice said from directly behind Skylar. "You poor, poor man."

Skylar wheeled around, her mouth an astonished O. "Must you keep repeating yourself?" she snapped, causing two middle-aged ladies to scurry like crazy toward a dark green sedan. She spun back around, the fire in her eyes leaving Logan in little doubt as to what was in store for him.

"Oh, you toad! You pig! You—you bastard!" she kept throwing out the names. "How could you do that to me? How could you?"

"Me?" Logan asked when he could get his breath again from laughing. He shook his head, wiping the tears from the back of his eyes with a white handkerchief. "I've never seen anything coincide so precisely. It was fantastic. You should have seen their faces. Better still, you should have seen *your* face."

Skylar stalked over to the passenger side of the Mercedes, got in, and slammed the door. She would not say another word to him. No matter if he were to drop at her feet, clutching his chest and gasping his last breath, she would not speak to him.

Logan slid behind the wheel, started the engine, and drove out of the parking lot. "Tell me about Amsley," he began.

Skylar stared straight ahead.

"How long has it been in your family?"

"Was it built by your ancestors or was it bought from someone else?"

"While you were taking a shower this morning, a friend of yours called. He wanted to know who I was. I told him I had moved in with you. Let's see, now, what was his name? Freddy . . . no. . . . Sam? . . . no. Ah, yes, I remember now. It was André. He appeared speechless at first, then wished us luck."

Skylar turned and stared at the imbecile driving the car. That's right, she told herself, a damned flaming imbecile! "You'd better be teasing, Logan Gant. André Costain happens to be a very good friend of mine. He's also a very dedicated gossip. Do you get my drift?"

"Oh, well," he retorted with suspect indifference. "What's to worry? With you not speaking to me, how can our relationship survive?"

The full implications of what could happen if he really had said any such thing to André rushed through her mind with all the finesse of a bulldozer. Dear Lord! André's uncle was on the hospital board with Aunt Katherine. "Please tell me you're teasing?"

Logan glanced at her, fully intending to make her suffer. But when he saw that she really was worried, he couldn't find it in his heart to continue the farce. "I didn't say we were living together," he said evenly. "But I did let him know in no uncertain manner that you were off limits to old boyfriends."

"And just who gave you the authority to run my life, Mr. Gant?"

"You did, Ms. Dennis," he came back swiftly. He even went so far as to pull the car over to the side of the highway. He cut the engine, then turned so that he was facing her, one arm resting on the steering wheel, the other one along the back of the seat. "Listen to me, Skylar Dennis, and listen good." His eyes were the most brilliant shade of blue she'd seen. In fact, she told herself, there was an electricity about him that was almost spooky.

"I want there to be no misunderstanding between us on this matter. Understand?" At the shake of her head he went on. "I was married once, many years ago. We were both in our early twenties—young and in love. We'd just learned we were to have a baby. If I were to tell you we had a lousy marriage and that I was miserable, I'd be a damned liar. Rather, we were deliriously happy. Our love . . . the prospect of having a child . . . I can't begin to explain what it all meant. Then it ended. One minute we were one, the next she was torn from me. Brutally—and unexpectedly. Iseult was laughing and talking with a friend, and not paying the slightest bit of attention to where she was going. She stepped off the curb and straight in front of an

248

oncoming car. The poor bugger who hit her was devastated. Till you, no other woman has meant anything to me. I've had one-night stands, I've had mistresses, I've had friends who became mistresses. But I've never had a 'lover' in that very special sense of the word—till I found you. And if God's willing, you'll be my last."

He stopped talking as abruptly as he'd begun. Skylar sat for a long, silent moment like a statue, just staring at him. For a brief instant she closed her eyes, emotion adding its own shimmery touch. She was bewildered. Another woman had held Logan's heart in her hand. She thought of the poor unborn baby—of a young, heartbroken Logan burying his lovely young wife, then lashing out at the world for the injustices it heaped on people.

He'd told her a little bit about his childhood, and she wanted to weep for him for the loneliness he'd known then. She'd lost her parents when she was a little girl, but there had been Aunt Katherine, always her Aunt Katherine, shielding her from the bitter existence a lonely little boy had had to bear alone. There'd been no one to take Logan and try to make it better. He'd been shifted from one foster home to the other till he struck out on his own. As he'd explained, it hadn't always been their fault. Most of them were very decent people. It was simply that he felt he didn't belong.

"I'm so sorry," she whispered through the tears blurring her vision. "So sorry."

He shook his head, then leaned over and brushed his lips against hers. Skylar thought he was smiling, but she really couldn't tell. "It's not pity I want from you, honey. I want your love. You say you love me now, and I honestly think you mean it. But, Skylar, there are degrees of love. We have some serious problems facing us. You have very firm convictions regarding my profession, and I have some very dedicated convictions. One in particular: I've started something, and I can't stop till it's finished."

Without his telling her, Skylar knew he was talking about the baldheaded man and the group with which he was associated. "What if it finishes you, Logan—what then?"

He didn't look away, and for that she was thankful. It had been almost weird, but from the very beginning, even on the plane during that first bizarre meeting, there'd been an element of honesty between them that later puzzled her. Of course there'd been Logan's disguise on the plane, but he'd explained it to her. Later, when he'd been wounded, he'd sought her out, knowing he could trust her. Would this simple honesty and trust they shared be strong enough to carry them through the coming weeks?

"I love you, Logan Gant."

"It's very soon after Tim, Skylar," he reminded her. "Take your time. There's no way I want to pressure you. You aren't obligated to say you love me, you know. Nothing's going to change the way I feel about you."

"How can I explain my feelings for Tim without you thinking of me as immature?"

"Try me."

"I knew Tim a couple of years before we ever went out together. I'd never known anyone as"—she raised her hands in a gesture of puzzlement—"I don't know how to explain him. With Tim you moved forty or fifty paces ahead of everyone else. When he wasn't on duty, we were constantly on the go. Looking back now, I can see that he was heading for a breakdown. There was no way in the world he could have gone on the way he was. I suppose one of the reasons I disliked his work so much was the way he went about it. If it was dangerous and life threatening, then Tim was all for it. Itching for a chance to get at it."

"I've known one or two like him."

"What happened to them?"

"The truth?"

"Please."

"One was killed in service—which is what

we call it when an agent dies in the field. The other one died on a mountain-climbing expedition—he was on vacation."

"The Tims of the world don't seem to fare too well, do they?" she said sadly.

"No, they don't," he said bluntly. "Unfortunate, but true."

"So you see, Logan, I have no problem with telling you that I love, because I do."

She honestly looked for him to take her in his arms at that point, but he didn't. Instead, he squeezed her hand lying on the seat beside his thigh. "Let's go see Amsley and Aunt Katherine. By the way, Skylar," he began silkily. "How long has Amsley been in your family?"

"Since the early eighteen hundreds."

"That must be very nice . . . knowing you are walking in the footprints of your ancestors."

"I must confess, I've never really stopped to think about it. It's just always 'been.' I dearly love the place, and help Aunt Katherine anytime she asks me to do something. But I suppose I've always been inclined to accept it."

"Will you inherit it when your aunt dies?"

"Yes. And that makes me very sad. Amsley without my Aunt Katherine is something I'm not ready to think about yet."

"Well, from what I saw of her yesterday, I'd

think you'll be spared for many years to come. Exactly how old is your aunt?"

"Seventy-eight."

A whistle of admiration pushed past Logan's lips. "She's quite a lady."

That same whistling noise came again as Logan drove from beneath the canopy of oaks and onto a slight rise upon which sat the simple yet striking beauty of Amsley. It waited like a small, proud queen, its lines clean and uncluttered, the grounds surrounding it neat as a pin, the flower beds perfectly laid out.

The Mercedes came to a halt at the front, only a few feet from the aged cypress steps. But instead of getting out, Logan just sat and stared and stared. It was incredible. The house, the grounds, Katherine Damler, and—he turned to look at her—Skylar. They belonged to each other. "I like your Amsley, honey."

"Tell Aunt Katherine that—after you get through discussing the Civil War. You'll be her friend for life," Skylar told him as she scooted across the seat and got out on his side.

As they rounded the car, the front door opened and Katherine came hurrying out to greet them. "It's about time," she fussed. Skylar ran ahead of Logan, in order to keep her aunt from coming down the steps. "I know why you did that, young lady. You must learn to stop pampering me." She waved her stick about. "I'm like old leather, tough and mean."

That began the usual banter that always took place between Skylar and Katherine. All during the afternoon and evening Logan watched them, laughing with them, at them, and sometimes merely staring—enjoying, envying the closeness they shared.

At Katherine's insistence Bernard took Logan down to the pond for some fishing. In their absence Katherine asked Skylar where she'd met Logan.

Without going into all the gory details Skylar related the story to her aunt. "I don't know if I can stand for him to leave, Aunt Katherine. It's coming, and there's nothing I can do to stop it."

"Try not to waste the time you have together by regretting what is to come, dear. If you stop and think about it, the future and what will happen is the essence of life. We can't escape it, no matter how hard we try. Your Logan is a very unique man, Skylar. He's strong and powerful and determined. He'll come back to you. Just believe, honey, believe."

But later, as they ate the delicious dinner served by Madeline, the housekeeper-cum-cook, Skylar found little comfort in her aunt's words. She watched Logan, watched him

254

pamper Aunt Katherine by indulging her with her favorite subject, the war, then saw him show nerve enough to disagree with her when he had opposite views on a particular subject. She secretly applauded him. There were very few men who dared disagree with Katherine Damler.

When they were ready to leave, Katherine drew Logan's head down and kissed him on the cheek. She placed a small hand on either arm and looked up at him. "My niece has told me a little bit about what you do, young man. It sounds like a grisly business, but I do realize it's a very necessary one. However, I'd like to think I'll have the privilege of seeing you seated at my table for dinner—many, many times in the future. What about it?"

"You keep the place set, Katherine Damler, and I'll be back, I promise."

Skylar was a little apprehensive on the return trip to New Orleans, wondering if Logan would be angry with her for having revealed his profession to Katherine. After worrying and worrying herself with the notion, she simply asked him, and was somewhat surprised by his reply.

"Not at all, honey. I seriously doubt your Aunt Katherine is going to squeal on me."

That night, their lovemaking was so perfect, Skylar cried afterward. She went to sleep in Logan's arms, only to dream of his being brutally wrenched from her. She awoke in the morning with dark circles beneath her eyes and a terrible headache. It was as if she hadn't even been to bed.

Logan made no comment on her physical appearance. When it was time for her to go to work, he drove her, promising to come back for lunch. "If you're late, I'll come after you," she teased, then waved and was gone.

They went to a small hole-in-the-wall type place for lunch. They ate thick, dark seafood gumbo and large buttery pieces of French bread, washed down with cold beer.

That evening they stayed in, watched a little television, then went to bed. The next morning, Logan and Allen met after Francine and Skylar had left for work.

"I think the time has come for us to get in position," Allen said quietly. "There've been no changes that we know of in any of the conferences, so we can only assume they're to go as scheduled."

Logan nodded. "I'll leave this afternoon."

"Knowing you as I do, I went ahead and bought your ticket." He handed Logan the envelope. "When we're finished with this particular project, there's something I'd like to discuss with you. Will you need me to drive you to the airport?"

"No, thanks," Logan assured him, "I've got my own transportation." He then checked the envelope for flight information. He stood. "If I'm to be on my way by three o'clock, then I'd better get packed."

"This is a nice surprise." Skylar smiled across the table at Logan. "You must have a guilty conscience," she murmured. Suddenly her brows shot upward and she turned slightly to the left as she observed him. "You haven't been moving furniture around again, have you?"

"I might have been." Logan chuckled. "What of it?"

"I'll take a baseball bat to you, that's what of it," she said sternly.

He reached across the white linen expanse and tweaked her pert nose. "I'm positive it's that great fear of bodily harm that keeps me in line, ma'am."

"Bull!"

"True." He shrugged, smiling. "But you're so delightful to tease." He took a sip of the Scotch-and-water he'd ordered, sat it down, then looked directly into her green eyes. "My plane leaves at three o'clock, Skylar."

Not a muscle moved in her face . . . in her entire body. Her hands, resting in her lap, became heavy as stone. The only noticeable change was her heart. It began racing like crazy. For one brief moment she honestly thought it was going to jump out of her chest.

"When did you find out?" Dear Lord, please! Don't let him go. But even as she uttered the silent prayer, she knew it was pointless. Nothing could stop Logan.

"I saw Allen this morning."

"Funny," Skylar said softly. "We've seen very little of him and Francine these last few days. Isn't it odd that they fell for each other so quickly?"

"Not really, Ms. Dennis," he smiled. "Have you considered our own relationship and how fast we found ourselves head over heels in love?"

She ducked her head, a sheepish grin on her lips. "I suppose all four of us sort of jumped the gun, didn't we?"

"Maybe . . . maybe not. We're all of an age when we should know our own minds. I know in my case it's certainly that way. I saw you, and I knew immediately that I liked you —though to be honest, on that plane, I didn't think I'd ever see you again."

"Oh, dear." Skylar feigned disappointment. "And all this time I thought you deliberately took my luggage so you could have a legitimate excuse for dropping by sometime."

"Hardly. People generally don't appreciate it when I drop by."

Skylar chuckled. "You can say that again, buster." And though her laugh sounded for all the world as normal as could be, only Logan detected the hollow ring. He knew, just as she knew, they were both playing a game—a game of pretense.

She was pretending that his abrupt announcement, that he was leaving in a little less than two hours, wasn't as painful as if someone had dealt her a stunning blow to the stomach. He was also pretending that his announcement of his imminent departure was as common and ordinary a thing as eating a bowl of soup or drinking the scotch and water before him.

They were both determined to carry out the farce, yet each was quietly dying inside . . . and each knew the other was feeling the same.

"Be sure and say good-bye to Katherine for me," Logan said with a smile. "You know, Skylar, I was astounded by the way you favor your aunt. You're very much alike."

"So I've been told. I think it pleases Aunt Katherine. She and Uncle Henry never had children. When she learned that my parents had requested in their will that the court appoint her my legal guardian, she was thrilled."

"She must have been very close to your . . . mother? . . . father?" He shook his head. "I'm sorry, but I'm afraid I never did understand which one it was she was related to."

"My mother. They were quite close. You see, Aunt Katherine was the youngest of seven children. In fact, the others were practically grown, and some were even married and had children, when she was born. That made her not quite young enough to be my great-aunt, yet too old to be just an aunt. We've always joked about her parents being rather startled by her arrival. It must have been disconcerting to dawdle a grandchild on one knee and your own baby on the other."

Logan grinned. "Frankly, I think your great-grandfather was a terrific old guy."

Skylar smiled coolly at him. "That's because you are a chauvinist pig, Logan Gant. I suspect Great-grand-mère considered him to be something of a sex maniac."

They laughed—nervously. Logan looked at his watch. Skylar clenched her fists so tightly, she could feel the tips of her nails biting into her skin.

When he walked out that door, she knew her heart was going to break.

But why? a small, hesitant voice asked. Why?

Because she felt he was never coming back, she acknowledged without batting an eye.

"It's time, honey."

She nodded. "I know. Remember that I love you."

"I will."

"You deliberately told me here, in the restaurant, didn't you?"

This time he nodded. "There could be no easy way for either of us, honey. Alone, we would have drawn it out till we were left bleeding. As it is, hopefully, we can part with a portion of our hearts intact."

"How long will you be gone?"

"Could be days, could be hours. I have no way of knowing."

"Can you tell me where you'll be going?"

He gave a defiant shake of his head. "No," he said firmly. "I don't want you knowing *anything* about where I'm going or why. It's safer that way."

Skylar didn't bother pointing out that it might be safer physically, but that emotionally it was just as dangerous. She watched him slowly rise to his feet, thinking she'd never seen him looking better. He was dressed in a navy blazer and light gray slacks. White shirt —sans tie—brought an involuntary smile to her lips. There were so many little things she would remember later.

"Good-bye, Skylar."

"Good-bye, Logan."

He turned and walked away, never looking back.

Joey and Hubie, who had been casually observing the two, looked at each other in puzzlement. They could sense something was wrong, but not having heard the conversation, they had no idea what.

Finally, Joey walked over to the table. The place was empty after the heavy luncheon crowd, so he felt free to broach the subject of her obvious unhappiness. He pulled out a chair and sat down.

"If you'd rather be alone, honey, just say the word."

Skylar didn't even look at him; she was still staring unseeingly at the front entrance. "I'm so numb, Joey, I don't know what I want."

"He's gone?"

"Yes. He's gone."

"Did you two break up . . . have a spat? Or is he away on business?"

"You're terribly nosy." She finally looked at him.

"True, but it's because Hubie and I have a vested interest in you, you know. We're partners. That gives us special rights."

"You're a special nut, that's what you are. But to answer your question: Logan will be away for a while, and no, we haven't had a fight."

"You really do care for that guy, don't you?"

"With all my heart, Joey, with all my heart."

CHAPTER FOURTEEN

Logan held the hand sprayer over the mums, looking, for all intents and purposes, as if he were either fertilizing the plants or spraying them for insects. He was doing neither, however, but the position of the long flower bed afforded him an excellent view of the bungalow being used by one of the foreign delegation. Cal was looking after the other one, and Sean McDonald was assigned to the Americans.

Cal's voice suddenly broke the silence. "Anything going on over your way, Hawk?" They were wired, but only used the equipment when they were sure the one they were calling was alone. And though they were some distance apart, Cal could see Logan perfectly. They had small devices in their wristwatches that could be used when the occasion warranted.

Logan raised a hand to his forehead on the pretense of wiping sweat from his brow. "Not a thing, Apache, not a thing. These guys have been gone since around ten-thirty. They went on one of the tourist cruises. They aren't due to arrive back till close to six this evening. I'm taking a break to call Rainbow in a few minutes. Any messages?"

"Nothing."

"Position yourself so that you can keep an eye on both locations. Okay?"

"Will do."

A young kid, dressed in the same tan pants and shirt that Logan was wearing, came strolling by. "Hey, you," Logan called out. "Keep this sprayer on these mums till all the solution is gone."

"But I'm suppose to be getting a pair of shears for Ben," the young man told him.

"I'll get the shears for Ben. You take this sprayer," Logan told him in such a commanding voice, the order was obeyed without another word.

After rinsing off his hands at an outside faucet, Logan walked through the grounds, down a block, and across the street to a small liquor store. He went inside and to the back of the store, the position of the phone giving him an excellent view of the entrance and the street outside.

The minute Allen came on the line, Logan could tell something exciting had happened.

"What's up?" he asked.

"A stroke of pure genius," he was told enthusiastically. "I've practically walked a hole in the carpet waiting for you to call in."

"Let's have it."

"We've finally got something on the bald-headed character."

"And?"

"Remember the incident in New Orleans? Where he was involved in that little accident with the garbage truck?"

"I remember," Logan said harshly. Not only did he remember the "little accident," he would never forget the look of horror in Skylar's eyes when she realized what had almost happened to them.

"Well, it seems your friend became enraged —we can assume he was angry because he'd failed to wipe you out as ordered—and took a swing at a police officer. Naturally they obliged by carting him off to the local calaboose, at which place he was duly photographed and fingerprinted."

"Great!" Logan exclaimed. "Who's responsible for that great piece of detective work?"

"Actually, it was Susan who found out."

"Susan?" Logan chuckled. "You mean with all the advanced equipment at your disposal that's suppose to be able to ferret out a shadow from behind an impenetrable steel wall—not not to mention an army of highly trained specialists standing by—it was a secretary who cracked the case?"

"Don't rub it in, Hawk." Allen sighed. "I've been teased enough as it is. At any rate, she got the idea to go back over each detail in our possession, which were pitifully few, and that's what she came up with. Now," he said excitedly, "here's the kicker. Ever heard of Genesis?"

"God, yes. Who in our particular line of work hasn't heard of them? They don't even bother with the pretense of killing for a cause. Their cause is money—from the highest bidder. Is that what we're up against?"

"You got it, my friend."

"This could be a bad one, Rainbow."

"I know. Exercise extreme caution. Your friend should be showing up soon, if he hasn't already. His name is Conan Steinman—a German. He's fifty-two years old and an explosives expert. Get this. He served fifteen years in prison for killing his mother. And that was when he was seventeen years old. Said she annoyed him by making him clean his feet before coming in the house."

"Real pleasant guy, mmmm? By the way, how is the Lark?" Logan used the name he and Allen had given Skylar.

"From my last report that area was unduly

quiet, but coping. In general I'd say everything is fine."

As he walked back to the hotel, Logan found himself wanting to throw in the towel. He wanted to forget Conan Steinman and all the others like him. He wanted to hop a plane and fly straight into Skylar's arms. God! But he did miss her so much.

Before he reached the manicured grounds of the resort, Cal's voice cut in. "Hey, Hawk. Guess who's here?"

Logan froze. "Baldy?"

"In person. He just walked out onto a balcony on the second floor. As we speak, I'm getting an excellent view of him. He's pumping his arms as if taking some kind of deep-breathing exercise—else he thinks he's a stork and about to fly off."

"He's a bird all right, Cal, and a damned big one. We finally got a make on him."

"Let's have it." When Logan finished, Cal was just as amused as Logan had been that Susan was the one to have nailed Steinman. "Always thought that gal was wasted at a desk."

"Mmm-hm, Cal, my friend," Logan said mockingly. "We all know where she'd best serve your purpose, but I don't think Susan agrees."

"Give me time, Gant, give me time. If you

can make the grade, then there's hope for me."

"Okay," Logan grunted, "I'm back in position now." He slipped into the cool, dim overhang of the lone banyon tree on the grounds. Several had been planted, but only one survived. He reached into a hole in the tree and removed a pair of binoculars. After training them on the second floor he picked up the blurred outline of a man. His fingers adjusted the focus and the blunt, cruel features of Conan Steinman looked close enough to touch.

Cold, silent rage was stirred anew as he watched the brute of a man, watched him pumping his arms, then changing to knee bends. It was fascinating and repulsive at the same time.

On one particular movement of Steinman's hand Logan caught sight of something on the hairy side of his wrist. What was that? he wondered. He quickly dropped the glasses to ground level and sought out Cal, several hundred feet down the seemingly endless expanse of green, leaning against a tree.

"I just caught a glimpse of something on Steinman's right arm. Can you make it out?"

After a few minutes Cal came back. "I can't distinguish anything. Any specific reason?"

"Right before he died, Achmed tried to tell

270

me something. He was having a difficult time trying to breathe, but he managed to get out the words *ambassador, scarab,* and *assassination.*"

"Scarab? Sacred to ancient Egyptians," Cal muttered thoughtfully. Found in most ancient tombs. I wonder what the connection is?"

"From what I just saw, it has to be a tattoo on Steinman's wrist. Apparently Achmed already knew then what we've only found in the last few days. He knew about the assassination, who it would be, and by whom."

"Makes sense to me. We should know for sure real soon, man. The first meeting of the conference begins this evening. That's why it struck me as odd for that bunch on your end to go off sightseeing."

"Different strokes for different folks, my friend. Talk with you later." After informing Sean McDonald on the latest development Logan settled down to wait.

Time weighed heavily on the hands of each agent as minutes slipped into hours. However, during the lull, they instinctively prepared themselves for battle. Waiting wasn't an uncommon thing for them.

All was in readiness. The conference room had been wired with supersensitive bugging devices. McDonald was to be in the attic, in-

271

suring that no one had access to the room from that direction. That left the windows in the rear, covered by Cal, and the doors in the front watched by Logan, who was in the bungalow directly across the lawn and facing the room.

Eight o'clock. Logan watched the twelve to fourteen members of the three delegations arriving simultaneously, shaking hands and seeming to be genuinely fond of each other.

A snow job, he thought mockingly, nothing but a gigantic snow job. While they're posturing before each other with some bogus crap about peace, back in their countries, they're blowing up each other like it's the last day on earth. It made him a little sick to sit and watch the farce. If they were serious, then he sincerely hoped it worked. Unfortunately, he'd seen too many of such meetings for him to have a great deal of faith.

When nine-forty came, Logan heard the suggestion for coffee and sandwiches from the recorder sitting on the table to his right. The call was made, and Logan alerted the other two.

"This could be it. They've ordered coffee. There's no way of telling which way the waiters will come. Stay alert!"

He put his hand to his gun, then slipped like a shadow from the bungalow. Outside, he paused, still in the shadows, his eyes alert for any movement.

Suddenly the sliding glass doors of the conference room opened and the three delegations began spilling out onto the large terrace.

"Judas Priest!" Logan exclaimed in a harsh undertone. He raised his wrist to his mouth. "Careful, Cal. The whole damned bunch have decided to gather on the terrace. Got that, McDonald?"

Cal answered in the affirmative, and Logan crept closer, using the shadows of the numerous trees to shield his presence. He crouched on the ground, extensive study in preparation of the case enabling him to identify each of the people in the group.

What was bothering him at the moment, however, was that two men from one of the foreign delegations, the one friendly to the U.S., had become separated from the main body. They appeared to be arguing about something, and Logan wished to hell they would get their asses back where they belonged. Guarding one group was much easier than trying to protect two or three smaller ones.

The sight of two waiters pushing a loaded cart drew his attention.

"Looks like everything's under control," Cal remarked.

"Could be, could b—"

Logan's response was drowned out by the sound of a shot ringing out. He saw the American representative throw out his arms and go down on one knee.

"Hit it!" Logan yelled into the mike to Cal and McDonald. He threw himself onto the stretch of open lawn like a commando, pistol in his hand, his body crouched. The damned fools on the terrace would be sitting ducks if somebody didn't shake them out of their frozen state. "Take cover! Turn over the damned tables and get beneath them—anything!" he yelled at the startled group on the terrace.

"Behind you, Logan!" he heard Cal warning him, then felt a stinging sensation in his left arm. He began crawling for all he was worth toward the clump of palms that had served him so well in the last few days.

Strangely enough, though shots were going in all directions, Logan thought dazedly, he didn't hear a single human sound, other than the transmission of Cal's and Sean's voices.

"He's still behind you, Logan," Sean came on. "I've lost sight of him. I'm fixing to move up to the roof."

"Take care," Logan warned.

"How's that arm?" Cal asked.

"Burning like hell. How about circling to your left, Cal? Fire a couple of times and let

274

me get back in the heavy shadows. I feel as conspicuous as hell where I'm sitting."

"Can't say that I blame you. Okay, here goes."

Logan waited for the sound of gunfire, then began a sprint comparable to an Olympian effort. He hadn't taken more than two steps, however, when he heard the bullet whiz past his head. He dodged to the right, then to his left. Yet no matter which way he went, the bullets kept coming. He felt his right leg go out from beneath him, felt his chest hit the ground. Instead of lying still and waiting for the man to finish him off, he started crawling, using his elbows to pull himself the last few feet into the darkness of the trees.

Just as he was bracing his body on his good arm in preparation to stand, a heavily booted foot shot out, knocking his arm from under him and sending him sprawling to the ground. Logan looked up, straight into the face of Conan Steinman. He saw Steinman's evil grin, saw him raise the high-powered rifle to his shoulder.

Logan closed his eyes, willing the beautiful image of Skylar's face to pass before him. He thought of her in his arms, heard her soft whimper when they made love. I love you, my darling Skylar, he said silently as the gunshot rang out. But instead of feeling pain, Logan felt nothing . . . absolutely nothing.

He opened his eyes. Instead of Steinman looming over him, he saw the bottoms of heavy boots, toes digging into the earth. He looked beyond to where there was movement that turned into Cal, closely followed by McDonald. Both carried their weapons in their hands.

A motion from Cal cautioned Logan to remain perfectly still. He obeyed without the slightest thought of disagreeing. He was bleeding like a stuck pig from the two wounds, and he was terribly afraid he was about to pass out.

When it was ascertained that Conan Steinman's days as top hit man for Genesis was at an end, Logan stopped fighting. He had accomplished what he'd set out to do: with the help of Cal and McDonald and the entire Orka organization, Achmed's death had been avenged.

The day was one of those warm summer days that left a person feeling in a constant state of guilt. They knew they should be doing something worthwhile, but their bodies simply refused to obey such a heretical thought. Thus, they either sat beneath the shade of the low-limbed oaks in the comfortable swings, or they sat on the bank of the pond and fished, or they sat on the verandah of Amsley and allowed the recently installed ceiling fan to reduce the summer heat, creating a pleasant atmosphere for reflection.

"Logan Gant, you are suppose to be exercising." Skylar came out onto the verandah, her hands jammed on her hips, her forehead creased with worry. "I think we made a terrible mistake letting Aunt Katherine talk us into moving in with her. This place puts you to sleep. How do you ever expect to get well if you don't do what your doctor told you?"

A smile hovered around Logan's sensuous mouth as he peeped from his lashes at his wife. *Wife.* Each time he said the word he felt pride. They'd been married in the front parlor at Amsley, and Katherine had cried. Francine had made a beautiful maid of honor, Allen, a smiling best man, and Logan had acted like a complete zombie during the whole ceremony.

And soon, he figured, judging by the enormous bulge of her stomach and of course the doctor's predictions, he was going to be a father.

"Okay." She turned smartly away. "Lie on your lazy behind in that swing, if you want. When it comes time for your poor little baby to be born, I'll get Bernard to drive me to the hospital. That way, we won't interfere with you and your busy schedule."

"Skylar Gant, don't you dare turn away and leave me," he said gruffly. He swung his legs to the floor, grimacing as the swing caught the tender part of his calf through which the bullet had passed. From there it had torn a jagged path to his ankle, doing most of the damage in that particular joint, thus entailing long and painful hours of therapy and exercise.

Skylar was tempted to leave him sitting there, but when she looked at him, she was so thankful that he'd been spared, she had no choice but to walk into his waiting arms. She rested her forearms on his shoulders and laced her fingers behind his head. "You have become terribly spoiled," she told him. "This whole house is set to your every whim. When we go back to the ranch, I'm afraid you're in for a rude awakening. There'll be no Madeline to cook your favorite dishes, and no Bernard or Aunt Katherine to keep you amused."

They'd spent a couple of weeks at the ranch shortly after the wedding. And Skylar now understood the expression "Rocky Mountain High." She'd loved it. . . .

"They know a fantastic man when they see one," he teased her.

"I can't believe you said that. You've been

shot more times than a fox on opening hunt day. Every bone in your poor, tired, old body literally groans when you move, and all your joints creak. Really, Logan, you aren't in very good trade-in condition."

"Thinking of getting a newer model, eh?"

"Indeed yes. I'm going to need help raising these babies." She patted her stomach. "I've always been told that twins are a divine gift. And while I'm sure all that's well and good, it would be especially nice if their father could run and play with them. Which he could do, if he would do his exercises like he was told."

Logan pressed his face against the warmth of her breasts, inhaling the tantalizing scent of her body and the fragrance of the perfume she wore. In that position Skylar's stomach was riding against his chest. Sudden and strong movement had him jerking back as if shot. He watched the front of the soft yellow maternity sundress, and saw it move in several places at once.

"My children are very active today." He grinned up at his children's mother.

"So they are." Skylar smiled back at him. "They heard me lecturing you, and that's their way of adding their own weight to the argument. Very smart children we're having, Mr. Gant."

That evening after dinner, a dinner of which Skylar ate very little, she went to bed early. Logan played a quick game of checkers with Katherine, then went to check on her. The minute he walked into the room, every sense of normal, sane thinking took a quick hike through the window.

Skylar was standing by the closet, dressing. Every few minutes he could see her wince, then place her hands on her stomach and look at her watch.

"Er . . . I mean . . ." He cleared his throat and tried again. "Time . . ." He got out the word. "I . . . is it time for us to go?"

Skylar watched amused as he walked haltingly to the bed and sank down as if out of breath. She sighed. He was going to be absolutely no help at all. "Yes, Logan, it's time. I just spoke with the doctor. He said for me to get dressed and come on in."

He sprang from the bed as if new life had been pumped into him. He fairly sprinted across the room and caught her hand. "Let's go, then."

"Not yet, dear," she said patiently, disengaging her hand from his heavy clasp.

"Why not?" he looked harassed.

"Because I'm dressed only in my panties, bra, and slip. I don't have on my dress yet."

"Oh," he said foolishly. Skylar reached for the light blue dress and began pulling it over her head. She saw a sudden light appear in her husband's eyes and wondered what other bright idea had occurred to him. "Where's the suitcase?" he asked.

"Over there," she said, nodding toward the foot of the bed. "Now, if you'll zip up my dress, we can be on our way."

Four hours later Logan Matthew Gant and Katherine Francine Gant made their first appearance in the world. Babies and mother were fine. The father, however, who tried valiantly to stand by his wife during the natural childbirth, but who promptly fainted in the heat of the moment, was in a state of shock.

It was well into the next day before Logan, recovered and back to his old self, opened the door to Skylar's hospital room and quietly walked over to stand by the bed. He stared down at her, wondering for the umpteenth time what on earth he'd done to deserve her.

He reached out and touched her cheek, watching her move her mouth in an effort to scare away whatever it was tickling her skin. He wiggled his finger against the smooth skin. Her eyes opened. She smiled at him.

"Well, big girl, what have you got to say for yourself?" She caught his hand and carried it to her mouth, pressing her lips against his palm.

"Having babies is an awesome business." He grinned. "I fell like a redwood."

"I know," she recalled with a laugh. "To make it worse, nobody had time to do a single thing for you till later. We were too busy having babies."

"I'm so proud of you."

"Thank you. Did you go in to the office today?" He and Allen—who was now married to Francine—had retired from Orka and become partners. They had formed Gant and Deen Securities. It was going great guns, and Skylar and Francine were thrilled to death that their husbands were no longer associated with Orka.

"Yes. Allen is holding down the fort. He sends his love and will be by later this afternoon. The Cabots called from the ranch, said they could hardly wait for us to bring the twins out for some real Rocky Mountain air."

"Are you happy now, Logan?"

"More than I ever dreamed possible. And you?"

"Totally. You gave up Orka, I gave up the restaurant. We're going to have fun together, Logan Gant."

He kissed her long and tenderly. "We've

always had fun together, honey. That's one of the things I noticed first. God willing, we'll continue to do so for the rest of our lives."

"Amen."